Roses Are Red; He's Dead

Janet McNulty

This is a work of fiction. Names, characters, places, and incidents wither are the product of the author's imagination or are used ficti-tiously, and any resemblance to actual persons, living or dead, busi-ness establishments, events, or location is entirely coincidental. The publisher does not have any control over and does not assume any responsibility for author or third-party websites or their content.

Roses Are Red; He's Dead

Copyright © 2015 Janet McNulty
Cover Illustration by Robert Henry

ISBN-13: 978-1-941488-26-3
ISBN-10: 1941488269

Printed in the United States of America

—To all those who ever thought that trouble followed them.

Roses Are Red; He's Dead

Chapter  1

"May I open them now?" I asked Greg as I sat in the passenger seat of his car with my eyes shut.

Greg had been secretive for the last two weeks about this trip of ours, which he had planned with meticulous detail, saying that it was a big surprise. The closer we got to our destination, the harder it was for me to contain my excitement and curiosity. I felt the car slow a bit as he turned left onto a road riddled with potholes—some so large that they swallowed the tires.

"Not yet," he answered.

"Well, when may I?"

"In a moment."

The suspense was killing me. "You're not taking me to some creepy cabin in the woods are you?" I joked.

"No," laughed Greg.

I fidgeted in my seat. I hated being left in the dark.

"Okay, now you can open them."

I squinted a bit as my eyes adjusted to the brightness of the sun reflecting on the crystalline snow. Greg had brought us to what looked like a luxurious bed and breakfast for our getaway vacation. The homely building had two floors, with a quant setting and log cabin appeal. Though small, it looked like it could be a comfortable place for a romantic setting. A sign hung from the overhang of the porch with the words "Emily's Spa/Resort". The exterior possessed that quaint and at-home feel, but as we drove along the winding driveway, I noticed that the building was much larger than the front side had indicated.

"What is this place?" I asked Greg.

"It's a resort, of sorts," said Greg. "It started out as a bed and breakfast, but later they expanded. See those trees over there? There is a hiking trail that goes through there."

"How did you find this place?"

"An internet search." Greg parked the car. "I know we have both been very busy with school and work and everything, so I figured we could use a nice break."

The one thing that Greg didn't mention was the fact that I tend to get involved in murder cases. Not that I ever wanted to, but it just sort of happens. Of course, it all started when I met Rachel: a ghost who had rented my apartment before Jackie and I had moved in. She had been murdered a year earlier and enlisted my help to catch the killer. Ever since then, ghosts just seem to show up at my front door—so to speak—wanting my help and I needed a break. Being Valentine's Day weekend, I had to commend Greg for planning this entire weekend without my knowing about it. The only thing I knew was that we were going away, but I had no idea where, or for what. Though, I think Jackie almost spilled the beans a few times.

"I hope you like it," said Greg as he got our luggage from the trunk of the car.

I looked around at the out of the way area. It looked peaceful. "You did good," I told him.

I took my suitcase and helped Greg carry the bags through the oak doors that led into a modern, with some antique chairs in the center, decorated place that was much larger on the inside than the exterior indicated. To the far right, rested the check-in counter with a middle-aged woman tending it.

"Checking in?" she said.

"Yes," replied Greg. "We have a reservation. Here's all of the information." Greg handed her a print out of the reservations he had made.

The woman took the paper with her boney fingers; her mouth scrunched a bit as she studied it, typing the reservation number into the computer. She leaned in closer to read the screen. "Ah, here you are. Just the two of you?"

"Yes," replied Greg.

"How nice," said the woman. "We get a lot of young couples up here like you two. Been together long?"

"A couple of years," I said.

A satisfied smile crept across her face. "I'm Emily and I own this place. Now don't let this small lobby fool you. We have the entire wooded area behind the building. There are hiking trails, a pond with ducks in it, and a nice grassy common area where you can lounge or mingle with other guests. We even have a spa."

"A spa?" I asked, my shoulder suddenly feeling stiff from all of the work I had been doing lately.

"Yes, here," Emily pulled out a map. "We are here. The spa is this building here. You can have this." She handed me the map.

"Thank you."

"Here are your keys. You will be in this building."

"Building?" I asked.

"Oh, yes, you had reserved one of our cabins."

"I thought this was just a bed and breakfast," I whispered.

"Oh, we started out that way, but as business picked up, I decided to expand. People seem to like resorts; and more customers you know."

"Thank you," said Greg, taking the keys and handing me the map.

"Just go out that door and turn to your left," said Emily.

Greg thanked her again.

"Enjoy your stay, dears," Emily waved and smiled before turning to help another customer.

I followed Greg outside the door that Emily had pointed us to. A huge wooden deck greeted us with lounge chairs—most of them with an occupant—and tables. Steps led to the grassy area. I was surprised that it actually had green grass on it with all of the snow around. A man on a bobcat clearing the snow from a nearby walk told me how they had managed it.

It actually felt warmer in this area compared to the parking lot, almost as though it was somehow temperature controlled. A glint of glass caught my eye. On closer inspection, I noticed it was a thermostat.

"These decks are heated," said a man, dressed in a white, polo shirt with the resort's logo on the upper left side just below the shoulder.

"What?" I asked, startled.

"Heated," said the man. "You know how some people have heated floors in their homes. Well, Emily decided to have heated decks. Wires run through the ceramic flooring, keeping it at a constant 70 degrees. Oh, it's perfectly safe," he added when he noticed my doubtful look. "That is why the grass is green down there. Panels lay underneath the dirt, keeping it warm enough to support the growth of the grass. And Joe out there has the lovely job of clearing the snow."

I surveyed at the man on the bobcat. "But this looks like real wood."

"It's supposed to."

I glanced at the people lounging on the deck underneath the heating lamps that were spread throughout. It did feel warm, despite the snow.

"Emily likes to make it as summer-like as she can out here, hence the panels and the heating lamps. I'm telling you, I never have to wear my coat on this deck. Of course, once you leave it, you'll wish you had one."

"Mel," said Greg.

"Oh, I'm sorry. I should have introduced myself," said the man. "My name is Chad."

"Mel," I said, shaking his hand, "and this is, Greg."

"Pleased to meet you," said Greg. "Mel, we should get going."

"Oh, what cabin are you in?" asked Chad.

"12," said Greg.

"That's it right down there. Those stairs will take you to the path that will lead you right to it."

"Thanks," I said. "Do you work here?"

"Guilty," replied Chad. "I'm in charge of making sure that the deck stays clean and the clients are happy. If you need anything, just ask."

"I will. Thanks."

Chad waved and hurried over to a woman on a lounge chair who wanted a refill on her drink.

I followed Greg down the stairs with our bags. With it being heated, there wasn't a patch of ice on the deck and I really wanted to take off my coat. At least, now I knew why everyone only wore shirt sleeves or a sweater. The path was where Chad said it would be, a nice paved stone with little marbles on the surface adding some character.

The little, wood cabin looked ornate with smoke coming out of the chimney and tiny, frosted windows on the sides. A small flower box lay in one of the windows; of course, there weren't any flowers in it, but that didn't bother me.

Greg swiped the key card in the slot on the door. The light turned green and the door popped open. "Looks old-fashioned, but still uses modern technology," he said.

We walked inside and turned on a lamp. A fire blazed in the fireplace. It was one of those gas fireplaces controlled with a remote. Someone must have turned it on just before our arrival. The cabin that looked small on the outside was actually bigger on the inside with its layout. The entrance opened into a nice living area with a kitchenette. A T.V. hung on one wall with a couch and chair in front of it. There was even a coffee table with a vase and some fake flowers. I opened one of the cabinets in the kitchenette. It had a few pots and pans and a dish set that served four. Glasses were in another cabinet.

"Well, if they have a grocery store we can cook our own meals," I said.

"They do," replied Greg. "There's a small grocery about a quarter of a mile away and a nice walking path that leads right to it."

"Of course," I mumbled, but it didn't surprise me.

I took my suitcase into the bedroom. A very comfortable looking king-sized bed lay in there with a thick, down comforter and fluffy pillows twice the size of what I had at home. A door on my right led to the bathroom. "This is really nice," I said, plopping my suitcase on the bed. A dresser sat next to the wall with a chair.

"It is, isn't it?"

"How much does this all cost?"

"Now don't you worry about it," said Greg. "It's all paid for with money I had been saving up just for this occasion. I thought we could use a nice weekend away. No classes. No work. No ghosts."

I chuckled at that last part.

"Seriously, though, no ghosts," said Greg. "Rachel doesn't know where we are does she?"

"No," I replied, "I made certain that only Jackie knew we were going away for the weekend. But you know how ghosts are. They always seem to find stuff out."

Greg grimaced at that.

"Look, let's just have a good time and not think about it," I said, as I unpacked my bag and put my clothes in the dresser and closet. I noticed Greg pull something small, and rectangular, out of his luggage. When he noticed me watching, he shoved it in his pocket and turned away. Though curious, I didn't press the matter. I guess every man has his secrets and it probably wasn't important anyway. Shrugging it off, I continued unpacking and tore off my coat.

A knock sounded at the door. Who could that be? I walked over to the front door and opened it. A woman stood there with a fruit basket. "Sorry to bother you, ma'am," she said, "but I forgot to put this in here this morning when I cleaned the room."

"That's okay," I said, taking the basket.

"I was hoping to get here before you checked in."

"Don't worry about it," I told her.

"If you need any extra towels, toiletries, or anything, just let me know. You can dial nine on the phone there to reach room service and dial eight to reach the maid's service; that's me."

I glanced over at a table in the corner of the living room that had a simple touch tone phone. "Sure. I'll do that. And thanks for the basket."

The woman walked off, pleased that I wasn't angry about her forgetfulness. A man loitered on the stone path. He seemed to be studying me. I couldn't place it; something about him seemed off, but I ignored it since this was Greg's and mine's weekend to relax.

"Who was that?" asked Greg when I closed the door.

"Just the maid," I said. "She forgot to set this in here."

I placed the fruit basket on the kitchen counter. The fruit looked delicious so I helped myself to an apple. The crunch and juice in it was just what I needed.

Chapter 2

I finished my apple and pulled out the brochure. They had a spa and it was open from six in the morning until nine at night. I knew exactly what I wanted to do. "Greg, I think I'll go to the spa. You don't mind do you?"

"Nah, go ahead," he replied. "Get that tension in your neck worked out." He rubbed my shoulders a bit.

"Thanks," I said. "I'll see you for supper." I pecked him on the cheek.

"It's at seven."

I waved at Greg, grabbed my key card, and headed off to the spa. The past few weeks, I had built up a lot of stress and my shoulders and neck constantly ached. The spa was brightly decorated with big windows to allow as much sunlight in as possible. Flowers lined the walls—

real, not fake—providing a fresh aroma, which I found enticing and suddenly wished that spring would arrive. I was so sick of snow.

"Hello, may I help you?" asked he lady behind the desk.

"Yes, I was wondering if I could get a massage? Do I need to make an appointment or…"

"Oh, not at all. Everything around here is available to our guests; no appointment necessary. I just need your name."

"Mel."

"Is this your first massage?"

"Yes." I could just imagine the look on Jackie's face if she saw me here getting signed up for a massage. She usually had to drag me to a salon to get my nails and hair done.

"Okay, Mel, if you'll follow me."

I followed the lady to the back of the parlor where she took me to a private room. The place was inviting with its soft lighting that accentuated the wood floor and walls.

"There is a bathrobe and some towels there. You just help yourself. Someone will be in with you in a moment."

"Thanks," I said.

I dropped my stuff and undressed, wrapping one of the towels around myself. The table I laid on had a velvety, plush cushion that hugged my body as I sunk into it enticing me to fall asleep.

"Mel?" said a voice as someone walked in.

"Yes," I said, sitting up.

"I'm Mindy."

"Good to meet you."

"Is this your first massage?"

"Yes."

"Any aches and pains you want me to work on?"

"My neck and shoulders have been really tense lately."

"Okay, well let's have you lie down."

I found myself descending into a world or bliss and relaxation. For a small person, Mindy had some strong fingers. She used lavender oil on my back; the scent filled my nostrils, making me relax even more. I must say, I should have done this earlier. Greg knew what he was doing when he had us come up here.

"You have a lot of tension in your shoulders," said Mindy. "Do you have a stressful job?"

"Not really," I replied, feeling even more relaxed. "I work at a local candle store, but I also go to school full-time at the university."

"Oh. Just starting?"

"No, it's my third year. I hope to graduate next May with a degree in filmmaking."

"That's cool. You want to direct movies?"

"Yeah," I said. This is the most I talked to any stranger. "I like making films. Short movies, documentaries—that sort of thing."

"That's really neat. Maybe you can get in on the Sundance Film Festival."

I laughed. "Not likely."

"You never know. Though you might want to take it easy next semester. All work and no play can lead to a very stressful life."

"Yeah." I was not about to tell her that I also tend to get visited by ghosts who want me to solve their murder or some mystery. That is a great way to get locked up in the nuthouse. "Guess I ought to take it easy sometime."

"You here alone?"

"No, I'm here with my boyfriend. He brought me up as a surprise."

"How nice. We get a lot of couples up here."

I found myself growing sleepy. This was exactly what I needed.

"Mindy," came a voice through the intercom, "please come to the front desk."

Mindy sighed. "I'm so sorry about this. One of our masseuses called in sick. I'll be right back."

I told her not to worry about it. I felt so comfortable that I just figured I would take a short nap. Unfortunately, relaxation was not to stay. A small noise sounded outside the door. I ignored it, sure that it was just someone walking past. It happened again.

Perturbed, I sat up, hoping that it would go away. The same sound happened a third time, but more insistent. Moaning, I stood up and approached the door. Thinking that maybe I should let it go, I almost turned away, but the same sound rattled the door for a fourth time. I opened it. A man leaned back in a chair—his head lolled to the side as though he were asleep—in the hallway. Something was wrong.

"Sir?"

No response.

"Sir?" I said, moving closer, while hugging the cotton towel to my body.

Eerie silence. Something was definitely wrong and that prickly feeling you get on the back of your neck struck me.

"Sir?" I touched his shoulder. He flopped over and crashed to the floor, unmoving.

In a bit of a panic, I ran to the front desk, my bare feet slapping the wood floor, while I clutched my towel. "He's dead!"

Heads turned in my direction as I entered the lobby area as a group of girls walked in.

"You need to get some paramedics or something," I said, breathless. "There's a dead guy back there."

"Ma'am, you need to calm down," said the lady at the desk.

"I am calm," I said, "but there is guy in the back and he is not breathing." I stopped speaking as I realized that all I wore was a towel, and there were an awful lot of people in the lobby staring at me. I wrapped my towel tighter.

"Call security," said the gal at the front desk.

Within moments, security showed up and I led them to where I had found the body and stopped short. It had gone. Nothing was there; not one sign of a body having been there.

"Where is he?" asked one of the security guards.

"He was right here," I said, moving closer.

Everyone looked at me as though I was crazy.

"I swear!" I had a throwback to the Christmas parade a year earlier, where I witnessed a woman get murdered and no one believed me because we found no body. What was going on here? I know I saw a man sitting in that chair and he was anything, but alive. "I'm not lying!"

"No one said you were," said one of the men present, "but there is no one here."

"I know there was a man in that chair. I approached him when he didn't respond and then he fell over."

"Are you sure he wasn't just sleeping?"

"I know a dead body when I see one." The moment those words exited my mouth, I wished I hadn't said them. The guard's eyebrows raised. "Look, he wasn't breathing."

"We'll search the premises, but is it possible that you imagined it?"

I stood my ground. Not likely.

"People here sometimes nap and when they wake up, they think something happened when it didn't."

Okay, so I had been dozing a little, but that wouldn't explain the body. Something didn't add up. "Perhaps," I relented, knowing I was not getting anywhere with those surrounding me. "I'm going to get dressed."

I went back into the room and put on my clothes. So much for a relaxing massage. As I reentered the lobby, everyone stared at me. They must have thought I was nuts; even I wondered if I was, but I know I hadn't imagined it. Security reiterated that they found no body and that there was no cause for alarm. Just the mistake of someone who had had too much of the perfumed oils. Mortified, I left, walking back to the cabin, hoping no one saw me and that I didn't get us kicked out. That would have been a great way to repay Greg's hard work on this romantic getaway.

"Hey," said Greg as I walked through the door. "How'd it go?"

"Not good," I replied.

"Oh?"

"I saw a dead body an—"

"Oh, no!"

"It's not like I set out to find these things. But the guy was gone by the time help arrived."

"I thought he was dead."

"He was."

"But dead people don't…"

"Get up and walk away, I know. They said I imagined it and now everyone thinks I'm crazy."

"I don't think you are," Greg hugged me.

"Maybe I did imagine it," I mumbled.

"They didn't find anyone, right?"

"No."

"So, it could have been a trick of your mind. You have been a bit stressed lately and sometimes the mind plays tricks when it's tired."

"You're right."

"Anyway, I got us reservations at the gourmet restaurant here. They are at seven."

I kissed him. "You're too good to me."

"I know I am." Greg wrapped me in his muscular arms and held me close. "How about we visit the hot tub they have here and work up an appetite."

As much as I wanted to, finding that man at the spa, and then having him disappear, rattled me a little, besides piquing my curiosity. Dead bodies don't just vanish into thin air and I wanted to know why this one had.

"Rain check?" I said. "I think I need to get some fresh air. And it will give me a chance to find some interesting things for us to do tomorrow."

"As long as it doesn't involve ghost hunting."

"It won't." I wasn't planning on finding any ghosts. I just wanted to make certain that I hadn't imagined the man at the spa.

I wandered around on the deck past the occupied lounge chairs as people lay in them, expecting to get a tan even though it was still winter. Still marveling at the how they managed to keep the outside deck and patio are so warm, I examined one of the floor panels.

"You lose something?" a woman asked me.

I looked up, imagining how stupid I looked, crouched on my hands and knees, running my fingers over the smooth deck floor. "Yeah," I said, "but it seems to have disappeared."

"Oh? What was it? Maybe I can help you find it?"

I rose to my feet, brushing my hands on my jeans. "No, that's okay. It was only an earring—costume jewelry. Nothing special."

"Better that than some expensive ring your boyfriend got you."

I gave the woman a quizzical look. She shook her dirty-blonde hair, allowing it to brush her shoulders with each wave.

"My boyfriend bought me a very expensive ring—diamond, you know—and I accidentally flushed it down the toilet. So embarrassing!"

"That stinks," I said.

"Yeah, no kidding," replied the woman, bunching her cashmere wrap around her shoulders.

"So are you here with your boyfriend?" I asked.

"Yeah, that's him over there." She pointed at a man

wearing a white, turtleneck sweater and sunglasses, getting two drinks from the outdoor bar. His chiseled jaw screamed gorgeous and his jet black hair complimented the woman's blonde. "Patrick!"

The man smiled and walked over, while dodging the oblivious crowd. I had to commend him on not spilling a single drop of their drinks as he navigated the crowd and before reaching us.

"This is Patrick," said the woman, "my other half. And I'm Aimie."

"Mel," I said.

"Well, Mel, nice to meet you. Oh, look it rhymes!"

We chuckled at that. People were always making rhymes with my name.

"Are you here alone?" asked Patrick.

"No," I replied, "Greg, my boyfriend, is in our cabin, resting. I just wanted to get some fresh air and explore a little bit."

"This place is amazing, isn't it?" said Aimie. "Here we are in the middle of February and we're not even wearing coats. I think it's great how they manage to keep this deck heated so you can enjoy yourself."

"What about that grass over there?" added Patrick. "Bet you never thought you would see that in winter."

"Not normally," I said.

"We should sit down," Aimie suggested.

"Yeah, here," said Patrick, handing her a drink. "Do you want one?" he asked me.

"No, I'm fine," I said. Before I knew it, the other drink had been shoved into my hand.

"There are some chairs over there," said Patrick. "You two go get them and take the drinks. I'll go get another."

Aimie and I did as Patrick had suggested, not that we needed much persuading. We found three lounge chairs and moved them closer together, forming a circle. I sank into the white cushions and marveled at how soft it was. Normally, when you sit in a lounge chair, you can still feel the bars through the cushions, but not on this one. Its pillow must have been three times as thick, and ten times more comfortable. Patrick came back within minutes with another drink—the same kind as Aimie's and mine—in his hand.

"Is this your first time here?" asked Aimie.

"Yes," I said. "Greg planned the trip for us as a get-away vacation. We had both been working hard lately and needed a break."

"This is the place to do it," said Patrick.

"This is our second stay," added Aimie.

"Really?" I asked.

"Our first visit here was great," said Aimie, "but we felt like we didn't get as much out of it as we could. So we came back."

"Best decision we ever made," said Patrick. "There is so much to do here."

"Tell me about." I leaned closer. "I am trying to come up with some activities for Greg and I."

"Well, for starters," said Aimie, "there is the 'Lover's Hiking Trail'."

"More of a nickname," chuckled Patrick, "but it does seem to live up to it. There are a lot of out of the way places it takes you to."

"Places where you and your boyfriend can be totally alone," Aimie said with a hint of scandal in her voice. "There is also the sauna. They have individual stalls for couples, and don't worry, they're soundproof." She winked at me.

"And," said Patrick, "there is a town only a quarter of a mile from here. They have a wonderful restaurant there that serves real Indian food; I mean, from India. The owner is a marvelous gentleman who loves entertaining couples."

"Tomorrow there's a couple's yoga," said Aimie. "You should come!"

"Couple's yoga?" I said.

"Uh-huh. They do all sorts of couple's things around here. In the morning, they have yoga, in the evenings, they have karaoke—oh, you gotta come to that. They also have live band concerts sometimes, star gazing, and they always have places you can go to be alone."

"I just might take you up on that yoga," I said. Movement in the corner of my eye made me glance to my right. Standing in a doorway, was the same man I had seen in the spa, except he looked a bit transparent.

"Something wrong?" asked Aimie.

I jerked out of my internal musing and realized that I had been staring at the same doorway for over a minute. "Fine. Everything's fine. I just thought I saw something, that's all."

"Oh."

"Well, I better finish my walk and get back to Greg," I said. I fiddled with my empty glass, unsure of where to put it.

"Here," Patrick took it from me and held it in the air. Within seconds, a man in a white outfit took it. "See? They don't want anyone to have to do too much work around here."

I smiled. "See you tomorrow?"

"Looking forward to it," said Aimie.

I left the two of them and hurried over to the doorway, but the man had gone. I almost stopped when I stepped through it and into a room the size of a dining hall with a humongous fireplace in the center—complete with the dancing flames—and plush sofas and chairs surrounding it. High, vaulted ceilings stretched above me with triangular windows that let in the sunlight. A chandelier of antlers hung from the rafters, releasing a soft glow.

A lump on one of the couches caught my attention. I moseyed over to it, thinking that maybe someone had left a blanket behind, or had fallen asleep; it was warm and cozy. As I neared the lump, something didn't feel right. Once again, the hair on the back of my neck stood up and the sensation that I was not going to like what I found struck. The lump came into view and I realized that it wasn't a lump at all, but the same man whom I had found in the spa. I looked around. I was the only one in the room.

"Sir?" I said. "I think you need to wake up."

Nothing. No snoring even; another telltale sign that something was amiss. "Uh, sir, this isn't funny."

Still no answer. I reached out to shake him away, but jerked my hand back as I remembered the incident in the spa. With great hesitation, I summoned the courage to shake him. As though determined to repeat what had happened earlier that day, the man fell over, his arms flopping out to the side as his head rolled to an unnatural position. I jumped back. It was the same man, and he was not breathing.

Turning in circles, I searched for anyone who might be able to help me, but found no one. I stood in the room, staring at the dead man before me. I knew I should go get someone, but it didn't work out so well the first time. Just to make certain that he was really dead, and not sleeping, I nudged him with my foot. Still no response.

I ran outside. The moment I opened the door, I flagged down the first person I saw. "Hey, there's…" I stopped. I had glanced back at the sofa and the body had gone with no trace of having ever been there.

"May I help you, ma'am?" asked the waiter I had flagged down.

"No," I said, puzzled as to what had just happened. "No, I forgot what I wanted, but perhaps you could tell me where the sauna is."

"Yes, it's down that way and to your left. You can't miss it."

"Thanks," I mumbled.

I looked back at the couch where I had seen the man, but it was empty. Confused, and a bit unnerved, I headed back to the cabin. The sun had sunk low in the sky and it would get dark at any minute. I still needed to shower and did not wish to be late for Greg's dinner plans. Maybe they would help me forget about this latest incident.

Chapter 3

The restaurant Greg had made reservations at was near the main part of the resort. I had to give him props for this. Not only was it an extremely nice place to eat an extravagant meal, with all of the fancy dishes one could imagine, but the calm atmosphere made me forget all about the spa and Mr. Not-So-Alive. A small lamp rested in the center of each covered table with an embroidered table cloth; the embroidery consisted of leaves and flowers woven together in small spirals along the hemline. Soft music played throughout the dining area.

The hostess seated us at a center table. I couldn't stop looking around at the décor. "Your waiter will be with you shortly," said the hostess.

"Thank you," said Greg.

I looked at the menu and almost gawked at the prices. "Greg, how can we afford this?"

"Don't worry about it," he replied. "I have spent the last several weeks saving up for this. Trust me. It's all taken care of."

I gave him a doubtful look. "You know you don't have to impress me."

"Of course I do," said Greg. "You're the super sleuth that solves mysteries ghosts can't solve on their own."

"Now you're just trying to flatter me."

"Is it working?"

"I'd say so."

"Good evening. My name is Matherson and I will be your server this evening. May I start you off with some wine?"

"Yes," said Greg, "we'll have your house wine."

"An excellent choice. Are you two ready to order, or do you need another moment?"

"I'd like your roast duck," I said. My stomach growled right then and I was certain that everyone heard it. "With the mashed potatoes and broccoli."

"And you, sir?" said the waiter to Greg.

"I'll have your prime rib."

"Excellent choice."

"With the baked potato and creamed corn," said Greg.

"I will put this in and your wine will be out shortly."

"So, Mr. Romantic, what's on the agenda for tomorrow?" I asked.

"They are having a couples hike tomorrow. Thought maybe we'd go there and figure out the rest later."

"Good thinking."

The waiter arrived with our wine. He poured two glasses and stuck the bottle in an ice bath on our table. I had to admit that the wine tasted good—I mean really good. It had a fruity flavor, but not overpowering, which I liked.

I reached over to grab a breadstick when my glass of wine fell over, spilling red liquid all over the table and the floor. A damp, red splotch coated a portion of my dress, which irritated me. Greg and I scrambled with our napkins to wipe up the mess, but we ended up making it worse. Our waiter rushed over with towels to sop up the spilt wine.

"Let me get that for you," he said as he tried to clean up the mess.

I couldn't believe that the wine had spilled. It seemed a bit strange that it had as I hadn't even touched the glass.

"Is there a place where I can clean up?" I asked.

"Yes, the restrooms are right over there."

I excused myself and went to the ladies' room. It had a sitting area that you had to pass through in order to get to the bathroom part. Using a bunch of paper towels and water, I tried, though with little success, to clean the wine out of my dress. Every effort I made just seemed to make the stain worse. Realizing that nothing I did would help the situation, I decided to just tough it out and spend the evening in a wine-stained dress. No point in running back to the cabin to change.

A scuffling noise sounded outside the bathroom door. I opened it and peeked out into the sitting area. A man sat on the couch, and he looked familiar.

"Excuse me," I said, "I think you're in the wrong room."

No response. Déjà vu hit me.

"Uh," I tried again, "this is the ladies' room. The men's is down the hall."

Still no response. An eerie feeling that I had been in this situation before filled me. Not again. I really didn't need this again.

"Hey," my tone grew more forceful as I approached him, "you need to leave."

Oh, yeah, he was unresponsive. Knowing I shouldn't, but I couldn't help myself, I reached out and poked him. He fell over, his face turning towards me and I recognized him as the man I had found in the spa and the lounge. I ran out of the bathroom.

"I need help!" I said to the first person I saw.

"What?"

"There is a man in there and he's not breathing," I said.

The man stared at me as though I was playing a prank on him.

"It's not a joke! There really is a dead guy in there."

The man followed me into the women's room, but wouldn't you know it, the body was gone. Gone! Again!

"So where is he?" asked the man.

"He was here," I stamped my foot. This was ridiculous! Why was I the only one finding a body—the same body—and then it disappears when I get help?

The man searched the sitting area of the restroom. Soon the door opened and a group of women walked in. Just what I needed: an audience. "Miss, there is no dead body here. Are you sure you didn't imagine it?'

"I know he was here!"

"Body?" One of the women ran out of the door screaming bloody murder. Great. Now I'd have an even bigger audience. Oh, sure, let's just bring the whole restaurant in.

The man looked at the wine stain on my dress and I knew he thought I had drunk a little too much.

"I'm not intoxicated," I said.

The look on his face indicated his disbelief. "Ma'am, there is no one here."

"But I know what I saw!"

"I need you to go back to your table."

"But…"

The manager walked in. "Is there a problem here?"

The woman who screamed bloody murder answered that question "She said there was a dead body in here!"

"She was mistaken," said the man who had investigated my claims.

"No, I wasn't!" The frustration in my voice intensified.

"Perhaps it was a man who mistakenly walked in," said the manager.

I looked around at everyone in the room. None of them believed me. "I know he was here!"

"Ma'am, I need you to return to your table."

"I won't…"

"Mel?" Greg had walked in, wondering why I hadn't come back yet. "What's going on?"

"Do you know her?" asked the manager.

"Yes, we came here together. She went to the bathroom and never came back."

"She insists that she saw a dead body."

"I did!" I reiterated.

"But there is no one here," said the manager.

"But…"

"Mel," Greg's voice silenced me; his eyes pleaded for me to remain quiet. He didn't believe me either.

I had lost this battle and I knew it. Once again, the body got up and left of its own accord and everyone thought I was crazy. I couldn't explain it and probably would never be able to.

"I must ask you two to leave," said the manager. "She's causing a scene and…"

"I understand," said Greg.

I read the disappointment in his voice. This was supposed to be a romantic getaway gift for me and I ruined it. Greg held his arm out to me and I took it, knowing that no matter what I did, no one would believe me.

"May we have our food packed in a to go box?" asked Greg.

"Certainly," said the manager, glad to be rid of us.

"Greg, I…"

He turned away. I had disappointed him.

"I'll meet you back at the cabin," I said and left the restaurant.

Fuming over the ruined dinner—and my part in it—I stormed out the door into the chilly, night air. The temperature controlled deck made it where I didn't feel the change, even though an icy breeze tickled my cheeks. Relishing the breeze, I stalked down the wooden steps to the walking trail below that wormed its way around the compound. Why was this dead body showing up only where I was, and then disappearing?

A rustling noise caught my attention. Knowing I shouldn't check it out, I kept walking. It happened again, this time, more insistent. Maybe I could just peek. No! No, I was not going to give in. My night was ruined enough.

It happened again. It was so loud and persistent that I jumped. Looking around, I didn't see anyone. Against my better judgment, I followed the noise. Wearing heels while walking on water soaked mud is not a good idea. Of course you're probably thinking, "Duh, Mel." But how was I to ignore it? Something strange was going on and I wanted to know what it was, and why it followed me.

Ignoring the fact that my nice shoes would need to be tossed, I pursued the persistent sound. I pulled back the branches of a shrub and there it was: the same dead body. Whistling drew nearer. I whirled around and found Chad walking towards me. When I turned back to the body, it had gone.

"Hey, Mel," said Chad.

"Hi," I muttered, still wondering where the corpse had gone.

"What are you doing here all alone?"

"I was just getting some air," I said, still bewildered about what had just occurred.

"Oh. I'll walk with you."

Since the body had disappeared, again, I knew there was no point in me telling anyone that I had found it, especially after the last two instances. "Thanks," I said.

"Are you sure everything is all right?" asked Chad. "You seem a bit rattled."

"Well, this weekend isn't turning out the way I wanted it to," I said.

"Oh?"

"Yeah. When I went to the spa I found a man that was slumped over. I could have sworn that he was dead, but when I got help he wasn't there."

"Embarrassing," said Chad.

"And just a few minutes ago, I could have sworn the same person was in the ladies' room at the restaurant over there."

"Did you tell anyone?"

"That's the thing. When I found someone, he had gone."

Chad got a pensive look on his face.

"You don't believe me."

"It's not that, but it sounds a bit fantastic, don't you think?"

"Yeah, that's what Greg said."

"Your boyfriend?"

"Yes, he's grabbing dinner."

"What did the man look like? The man you found."

"Well, he was short, somewhat bald, beer gut, and would give the zombies on The Walking Dead a run for their money," I replied.

"That sounds like Billy," said Chad. "He works around here—janitor. I would usually find him sweeping, or vacuuming the halls. He's the quiet type—not a lot of friends. Come to think of it, I haven't seen him lately."

"Really?"

"Not for a day or two. He could have just taken them off. Been known to do that. Disappear for a couple of days. Tell you what, I'll look into it, if you promise to quit finding dead bodies."

"Deal."

We said goodbye and I went back to the cabin.

Only a single lamp lit up the living room when I walked in, tossing my key on the table near the entrance with a loud plunk. Crunching footsteps alerted me that Greg approached. His erect and hurried demeanor indicated that he was in an irate mood, courtesy of me. The door opened and he stepped inside, shutting it with a bang.

"We can curl up on the couch and eat," I said, trying to brighten the dismal atmosphere.

Greg handed me the Styrofoam cartons that contained our supper. "I'm not hungry."

He went into the bedroom, turned on the light, and undid his tie. I watched as he tugged on it in exasperation, feeling guilty for ruining the perfect evening he had planned. I had lost my appetite as well. I shoved the food into the refrigerator and went to the bedroom. Greg had just finished brushing his teeth when I walked in. He said nothing. I decided it was best if I left him alone until he had cooled off.

I went into the bathroom and pulled off my earrings, while I turned the faucet on so that the water could heat up. As I scrubbed the makeup off my face, I heard Greg give a shout.

"What?" I said, walking out of the bathroom.

Greg stood next to the bed, holding the covers up, while lying on the mattress was the same corpse that had plagued me since we had first arrived.

"That's him!" I shouted. "That's the man that I keep finding. That's the corpse that keeps disappearing."

I snatched Greg's phone off the bedside table and snapped a picture, just in case the body vanished again. "We need to call the authorities before he up and disappears again."

"I'll go get someone," said Greg.

"No, you stay here. I'll go get someone."

"You had to go and ruin it," whined a male voice.

I stopped in my tracks and looked around. "Who said that?"

"Me, you idiot."

"Well, I can't see you," I said.

A figure appeared before Greg and I, and it looked just like the dead man in our bed, complete with the bear belly, poking through the stained, and washed out, shirt.

"I wanted only you to find my corpse," said the stranger, "but you had to go and ruin it by bringing in others. Now you have him involved." He pointed a stubby finger, with a chewed nail, at Greg.

"Well, I don't care if you're not happy," I snapped, placing my hand upon my hip. "You've been making me look foolish all day. I'm calling the cops."

"No, don't," pleaded the man. "I don't want their grubby, little hands all over what's left of me."

Ignoring him, I picked up the phone and dialed the lobby. "Yes, this is Mellow Summers in Cabin 12. I need to report a dead body... He's in my bed... No, it's not a prank. Look, just call the police and inform them that a murder has taken place."

I hung up and glanced at Greg. "Sorry," I mumbled.

The local police showed up within 15 minutes after I had contacted the front desk about the "guest" in our bed. Greg and I each threw on a pair of jeans; neither of us wanted to answer the door in our bedclothes. A harsh knock on our cabin door alerted us that they had arrived.

"Miss Summers," said the officer, as Greg opened the door.

"Right here," Greg said, pointing at me.

"You reported a dead body," said the officer.

"Yes," I replied. I led him and his partner into our bedroom where, thankfully, the body still remained. If it had disappeared again, I don't know what I would have told them.

Billy stamped his feet in the corner of our bedroom as the two officers walked in and checked the body. Soon a medical examiner arrived followed by paramedics. They investigated the body, took the liver temperature, and determined that the cause of death was most likely due to a severe blow to the back of the head; a conclusion that would be finalized back at the morgue.

"Do you know this man?" one of the officers asked Greg and I.

"Yes—yes, you do," said the ghost.

I did my best to ignore him. The last thing I needed was to be talking to a ghost, while being questioned by the police. That usually earns you a first class ticket to the psych ward.

"No," I said.

"Are you sure?" asked the officer.

"She said she didn't know him," Greg replied. "Neither of us saw him until tonight when we discovered him in our bed."

"Where were you yesterday afternoon?" asked the officer.

"What?" said Greg. "You don't think we did it, do you?"

"Sir, please just answer the question."

"We were back home, packing, and preparing for our trip here."

"Can anyone vouch for that?"

"Yeah, my boss," Greg snapped.

I placed a gentle hand on Greg to calm him down. "Officer," I said, "my employer can verify that I was at work yesterday afternoon. I have a roommate who can vouch for us, that we were with her last night. We did not arrive here until this afternoon. I am certain that you can talk with the lady who handles check-ins; she can verify our time of arrival." I gave the officer Mr. Stilton's phone number and Jackie's.

"Now, several eyewitnesses have said that you claimed to have found a body soon after your arrival," said the officer.

Uh-oh. I knew that my afternoon activities were going to come up. "I was at the spa earlier today, yes. While there, I thought I had seen a dead body, but it was gone when I managed to get help. Everyone told me that I had probably imagined the whole thing, and since I was a bit drowsy from the incense, I agreed with them."

The officer didn't believe me. "Witnesses say that you claimed to have found a dead body in the restaurant this evening."

There was no talking my way out of this. I had made a scene there. "Yes," I said. "I had spilt wine on my dress and went to the ladies room to clean myself up. While there, I saw a man slumped over and jumped to conclusions."

"An interesting series of events, considering that you now have a corpse in your bed."

"Now wait a minute," interrupted Greg.

"Excuse me," I said, "what are you insinuating?"

"Let's follow the chain of events, shall we? You claim to have found a dead body this afternoon and it disappears. Then, you claim to have found the same body this evening. Now, it shows up in your cabin, in your bed."

"That is an outrageous assumption," yelled someone from the crowd that had gathered outside our cabin. People moved aside as Patrick stepped out. "How dare you accuse her of murdering that poor man."

"I wasn't accu—"

"Oh, no?" said Patrick. "You sounded like you were.

"Sir, I must ask you to—"

"Maybe you should quit accusing her of placing the body in her own bed and find out who actually killed him and placed him there."

"Sir—"

"She was with my wife and me this afternoon and we saw them at the restaurant this evening. After a bit of commotion, she left."

"By yourself?" the officer turned towards me.

"Yes," I replied. "I came back here."

He gave me a suspicious look.

"I did run into Chad, an employee here, and he walked me to my cabin."

"A romantic meeting?" asked the officer.

"Now just…" I began, but Chad stepped out of the crowd and cut me off.

"No, it was not romantic. I saw her walking alone out here, looking upset, so I asked if there was anything I could do. It is my job to ensure that our guests are happy here. If I see one that is clearly not, I immediately ask them if there is anything I can do. It was strictly plutonic. Besides, I only walked her back to her cabin."

"Do you often walk strange women back to their cabins?" asked the officer.

"Yes, I do. It's my job to ensure their safety, as well as their happiness here. Honestly, officer, if you were in my position, would you have done any different?"

The officer didn't respond.

"He did it!" hissed the ghost in my ear. "Chad killed me. I know he did."

I shifted uncomfortably, trying to ignore him.

"You seem nervous," said the officer.

"Just tired," I replied.

"Of course she's tired!" shouted Patrick.

Aimie grabbed his arm and whispered something in his ear, probably to quiet him down before he got himself arrested.

"I am calm," he said to her.

A commotion arose as a plump little woman shoved her way to the front of the crowd. "Oh, dear! Oh dear!" Emily's graying hair squeezed out of the mass of gathered bodies. "What is going on here? Can't you hurry this up? I have a business to run and can't have a dead body around."

"Ma'am," replied the officer, "we're doing our job as fast as we can."

"Officer," said Greg, "we answered your questions. May we go now?"

"Yes," said the officer, "but remain available in case we have any further questions."

"Come with me," Emily led us away, back to the main

building, which had been the original bed and breakfast before the expansion. She pushed us inside and led us to the lobby, her flustered steps clacking on the floor as she walked. "Oh dear," she kept mumbling to herself.

"We don't want to be any trouble," said Greg.

"Oh, you're no trouble at all," said Emily.

"I'm telling you that that Chad guy killed me," said the ghost.

I glared at him, hoping that he got the message to shut his mouth.

"Oh, you're no bother at all," said Emily as she scrolled through screens on her computer. "But we do need to get you some new accommodations. Can't stay in that cabin. Oh, no. Ah, here we are. The honeymoon suite."

"We really don't…" I began, but she cut me off.

"No, no, don't worry about it." She entered some information on her computer. "It is our finest room. And no charge, really. In fact, I am going to refund your money."

"You don't need to," said Greg.

"I insist," Emily replied. "Finding a dead body in your room. How awful! No, this is on the house. Anything you wish, whether it's from the kitchens, the restaurant, or anything, charge it to the honeymoon suite and I'll take care of it."

"We don't want to be any trouble," said Greg.

"No trouble at all." Emily's face had turned red from the night's excitement, evidently afraid of being sued. "Ah, Chad."

Chad had walked in just as she handed us our key.

"Take them to the honeymoon suite—it's our finest room—and see to it that they have everything they need."

"Yes, ma'am," said Chad.

"Our things," said Greg.

"Oh, I'll have them brought to you once the police—dreadful thing, dreadful thing—are done. Yes, they'll be brought to you, don't you worry."

As I started to follow Chad to the honeymoon suite, Greg stayed behind, whispering to Emily. I watched him, wondering what he was up to. Emily's face went from flustered to overcome with joy as she hugged him and patted him on the back.

"What was that about?" I asked him.

"Nothing," said Greg. "Just wanted to make sure that all of our things would be delivered."

He held something back. I could feel it.

Chad led us through the lobby, and the large room with the gigantic fireplace in the center, to a door that led outside. As we walked, he stumbled and had to regain his balance. I glanced at the ghost, who still followed us, his guilt over tripping chad evident in his innocent expression.

The honeymoon suite was a cabin secluded from the rest of the resort, with a brick walk leading through the trees to it. I almost gawked when I saw it. Two floors with a beautiful awning and a front porch with a swing. Emily wasn't kidding when she said it was her finest accommodation.

"I think you two will like this place better," said Chad. "The second floor is the bedroom with a master bath." He opened the door and let us in, after which he handed the keys to Greg. "There is a powder room here, an indoor hot tub down there. There's a small kitchenette, but you can order all of the room service you wish. Just tell them to put it all on the honeymoon suite. Oh, and through here is your living room and a nice breakfast area that looks out onto the rest of the resort."

I stepped into the breakfast area with it luxurious bay window. The resort did look nice with its lights, though the police scurrying about detracted from the charm.

"The closet upstairs will have some things you can wear until we are able to get you your bags."

A knock sounded at the door. Chad opened it.

"Oh," said the same woman who had brought the fruit basket to our original cabin, "Chad, uh, Emily sent me with these: towels, toiletries, pillows, and extra blankets. I even have some night things for you to wear, from our clothing store."

"Bring them in," said Chad.

The woman rushed up the stairs to the master bedroom and came down five minutes later. "I do apologize for all of this," she said as she left. "Let me know if you need anything."

"She's a sweet girl, and will take good care of you, "said Chad. "Is there anything else you need before I go?"

"Yeah," spat the ghost; of course, only I heard him, "you can ask him why he killed me."

At that moment, my stomach growled. I tried to downplay it, but neither Greg, nor Chad would let me.

"I will have some sandwiches sent from the kitchen," said Chad as he left.

Chapter 4

The next morning, I awoke with a ray of sunlight peeking through the slit in the drawn curtains, stabbing me in the face. I crawled out of bed; the previous night's events were a blur, until I opened my eyes and saw Billy's fat face in front of me.

"Well, good morning," he said in a grumpy tone.

"Go away," I groaned. I was in no mood to talk to ghosts.

"You need to get dressed," he said.

"Oh, go haunt someone else," I replied.

"Well that's not very friendly."

"You've ruined my weekend with my boyfriend," I hissed at him.

"Oh, boo-hoo," said Billy. "We have a murder to solve. Mine."

"Who are you talking to?" said Greg as he sat up in the bed.

"You remember the body that was in our bed last night?" I said. "His ghost is here."

"Tell him to go away," said Greg.

"I tried."

I glared at Billy, not pleased that the one weekend I did not want to be bothered by a ghost, or another case of murder, was the one time I couldn't get rid of him.

A knock rattled our door. I hurried down the stairs to the main floor and opened it. Chad stood there.

"I'm sorry if I woke you," he said, "but I just wanted to check in on you and make certain that everything is all right."

"Oh, yeah, the room is great," I replied. "Would you like to come in?"

I opened the door wider, allowing Chad to step inside.

"Was the suite's temperature okay? If you need any more blankets or pillows, I can have them brought to you."

"We slept comfortably," I said. I could tell that Emily had sent him over to placate us in case we were angry over what had happened the night before, still afraid of suffering a lawsuit.

"That's him," hissed Billy in my ear. "That's my murderer."

I did my best to ignore him. Just then, Billy picked up a vase from a nearby side table and threatened to smash it over Chad's head while his back was turned. I rushed forward, snatching the vase out of thin air and jerking it downward away from Chad's head. He turned and faced me, giving me a quizzical look. I just smiled, while placing the vase back on its table.

"Are you okay?" he asked.

"Perfect," I said.

Billy crossed his arms and frowned at me. He spotted a paperweight on the coffee table and scooped it up—of course it looked as though it moved on its own as only I could see him—and approached Chad, paperweight raised. I darted around him, snatching the paperweight and tossing it behind me where it landed on the sofa with a soft plop.

"Are you sure you're all right?" asked Chad.

"Yes," I said.

Greg stomped down the steps at that moment, tying his robe closed. "Morning," he greeted us in a cheery tone.

"Morning," replied Chad. "I am just here to make sure that you both had a restful night. The cabin is comfortable?"

"Very much so," replied Greg.

I noticed movement in the corner of my eye. Glancing over, I saw Billy sneaking up behind Chad with a… lamp? What had gotten into him? I steered Chad towards the kitchen while motioning to Greg to look to his left. He saw the floating lamp. Greg dove over the railing for the lamp, grabbing it, trying to wrench it free of Billy's grasp. Before Chad was able to turn around, I yanked him further into the kitchen.

"The refrigerator seems to be running warm," I said, "and I can't figure out why."

While Chad opened the refrigerator and looked inside, I glanced back at Greg who still struggled with Billy for control of the lamp. They swung one another back and forth—Greg almost toppled over on two occasions—the lamp jerking with such violence that I was afraid they might break something. I cringed when the bottom of the lamp nicked the wall.

"What was that?" asked Chad.

"Nothing," I replied.

"Well, I found your problem."

"Oh?"

"This dial here"—he pointed at the temperature control on the side of the refrigerator—"was turned a bit too high. All you have to do is turn the knob and set it to the desired temperature."

"Thanks," I smiled at him, while blocking his view of Greg fighting over a lamp with an unseen force.

"I was wondering," I said, "how far is the grocery store you talked about. I wanted to get some things for us to eat."

"No problem," said Chad. "The store is only a quarter of a mile from here and there is a path down that way. It's been cleared of snow and has had fresh gravel laid on it. We also have a concierge service, that will go to the store for you and buy your groceries and deliver them to your room."

"That won't be necessary," I said.

Greg gave the lamp one final pull, freeing it from Billy's grasp and shoved it behind a corner, regaining his composure.

"Is there anything else I can help you with?" asked Chad.

"No," Greg and I said in unison.

Chad's face betrayed that he thought we were hiding something, which wasn't far from the truth, but never voiced his concerns. "I'll leave you to your day, then. Don't hesitate to let me know if you require anything else."

"We won't," I said, closing the door behind him. "Thanks."

Once the door had latched, I slumped against it, breathing a huge sigh of relief. "What were you thinking?" I demanded of Billy.

"He is the one who killed me," he replied.

"You don't know that," I said. "You, yourself, said that you didn't know who struck you on the head. You're just making false assumptions!"

"I am not," said Billy. "You just don't think he's not guilty because of his good looks."

I stared at him. True, Chad was drop dead gorgeous (dark hair, dreamy eyes), but that was not why I didn't think he had killed Billy. The truth was, there was no evidence pointing to any particular individual as the murderer. I looked at Greg who watched me shouting at thin air; his face told me that he hadn't heard Billy either.

Ghosts have the ability to decide who can see them and hear them, and who can't. Rachel, who was the first ghost I had ever met, routinely dropped by my apartment, uninvited, and announced her presence by popping in and popping out at will so that all could see her. I think she enjoyed such things a bit too much. But there had been other ghosts, like Billy, who preferred that only a certain individual communicated with them.

"Do you care to explain what is going on?" asked Greg.

"The corpse we found in our bed belongs to a former employee here named Billy," I said.

"And he is here, now," said Greg.

"Yes," I replied.

"So, why is he trying to hit the man that was just here with a lamp?"

"Billy, is convinced that Chad murdered him and he wants revenge."

"You have to help me," said Billy.

"Enough!" I yelled at him, growing irritated at his insistence that I help him put Chad in his grave. "I am not going to help you seek revenge."

Billy's face contorted in anger and he vanished. Relieved, though a bit worried about what he might do, I went back up the stairs to take a shower before breakfast.

Breakfast was uneventful, which was a relief, considering my entire stay so far had been anything but. We had gone to the only restaurant at the resort, and at Emily's insistence, had been allowed back in, despite the fact that the manager had kicked us out the night before. I looked at Greg as he sat across the table from me, wondering how I was going to tell him that our romantic getaway would have to be put on hold. He beat me to it.

"So, what's your next move?"

"Next move?" I asked.

Greg gave me his all-knowing look, informing me that I shouldn't play coy. "Mel, a dead body was found in our bed last night and the ghost of the man just tried to attack one of the employees here. You're not going to let this go, I know that. And the only way we will be able to enjoy the rest of our stay is if we find the one responsible for that man's death. Besides, I would like to know who put him in our bed in the first place."

"Oh, that would be Billy, the ghost himself," I replied, without thinking.

"What?"

"He wanted to get my attention."

"I'd say that it worked. So, what's the plan?"

"There is a couples yoga in about an hour," I said. "We could go to that. Not only will it look natural, but maybe we can glean some information from the other guests about Billy, if they knew him, or saw him around."

"I don't know if people will be talkative during a yoga session," said Greg as he sipped his coffee.

"Maybe not, but it is a place to start. Besides, yoga is supposed to be relaxing, and we could use a little bit of that."

"As long as your Aunt Ethel doesn't show up in leotards," quipped Greg.

I cringed as I remembered the time my aunt had shown up, unannounced, and tried to make us all do yoga, while dressed in polka-dotted leotards. "Promise," I said.

Couples yoga was held in a somewhat remote area of the compound on a small hill. The morning sunlight glowed on the mound of wilted grass, which had just been cleared of its blanket of snow, giving it a golden sheen. Though chilly, people didn't seem to mind the crispness of the air as they stretched, wearing nothing more than yoga pants and sweatshirts.

"Mel!"

I turned. Aimie waved at me as she bent over, touching her toes. I nudged Greg's arm and steered him over to where Aimie was.

"Hey," she greeted in a sing-song sort of way.

"Hi," I said, returning the greeting. "Where's Patrick?"

"Oh, he doesn't care for yoga," Aimie replied. "I know this is supposed to be couples yoga, but I don't think they are going to kick me out just because I am here by myself. I just never wake up completely, unless I have my morning yoga."

"I know what you mean," I said.

"Oh, but you managed to bring your boyfriend," exclaimed Aimie.

"Yeah, well," I replied, "I had to promise to do something he loves later on today."

"Oh, like what?" asked Aimie.

"Stargazing," said Greg, before I could respond.

"You don't like looking at the stars?" asked Aimie.

"Normally I do," I said, "but in the summer, when it's warmer."

"I'm sure there is a way you two can keep warm tonight, while staring at the stars," Aimie said, with a wink.

"Stop talking to me like that you old crone!"

We all turned towards the harsh voice behind us. It belonged to a man, who looked to be in his 60s, as he continued to berate his wife.

"Don't you call me an old crone you flabby old fart. You know, a few sit-ups, and a little less beer, wouldn't hurt you!" His wife put her hands on her hips, daring him to respond with a snappy comeback.

"One of these days, I am going to—"

"Oh, you've been saying that since the day I married your sorry butt."

We watched the two as they continued to berate one another. "Who are they?" I finally asked.

"Morgan and Burt," laughed Aimie. "The old, married couple around here. I overheard Emily congratulating them on their 35th year of marriage. Hard to believe, right?"

"Hello, everybody," said a female voice as the instructor arrived.

We all took our places, spreading out our mats.

"I know that it is a bit chilly this morning, but I think we will be okay," the instructor continued. "I want everyone to stand with their hands pressed together out in front of you, with your feet together. Breathe in slowly and exhale."

I glanced around as the people around me followed the instructions, each had their eyes closed, while meditating. Aimie seemed to be enjoying herself. Chad walked past the yoga group. Unable to stop myself, I allowed my gaze to follow him, wondering where he was going, but that was the least of my worries. A broken tree branch followed after him. I watched in astonishment as it floated after Chad, who remained unaware of the danger that trailed after him.

"Billy," I whispered to myself.

I couldn't see Billy—he was remaining invisible—but knew that he was the one with the tree branch. Why else, would a piece of wood be following after Chad?

While the others in the yoga class prepared for the downward dog pose, I bolted for the hovering tree branch. My shoes made squishy noises as I ran through the class, knocking a few of the attendees over in the process, focused on stopping Billy from whatever it was he planned to do. The broken tree branch raised higher into the air. My shoe caught on a mat just as I reached the edge of the cleared area and I stumbled forward, grabbing onto the hovering branch to stop myself from falling. My sudden impact forced the branch away from Chad.

Billy jerked the branch away from me, but I held on, tightening my grip. I tugged it away from him. In retaliation, Billy yanked hard, trying to hit Chad with the branch. I refused to let go. I planted my feet into the snow and leaned back, doing my best to maintain my balance as Billy jerked the branch in every direction in his attempt to free it from my grasp.

"Let me at him!" Billy yelled at me.

I refused. As splinters from the branch's bark dug into my skin, I gripped it harder, giving one last yank. Billy let go. I fell backward, landing on my rump with the snow forming a mound around me.

"I'll get him, yet!" shouted Billy, but only I heard him, thank goodness.

I dropped the branch. As I rose to my feet, brushing the snow off of me, I noticed the confused faces staring at me. "Uh…" I began.

"Mel, that was amazing!" said Greg as he ran up to me, giving me a hug. "Though I don't think this was the appropriate time for a spectacle, but those mime classes have really paid off."

"Mime classes?" I said to him, wondering what he was talking about.

"Just go with it," Greg whispered in my ear.

"What is going on here?" asked someone.

"You'll have to excuse us," began Greg, "but Mel has been learning how to be a mime and I guess she wanted to give us a show."

"That was interesting," Chad said before leaving.

"That was awesome!" said Aimie. "I almost believed that you were really struggling with someone."

"Thanks," I said, still catching my breath.

Judging by the looks on the faces surrounding me, I could tell that only half of them believed Greg's story.

"All right," said the instructor, irritated at having her class interrupted, "time to move into child's pose."

Greg helped me back to my mat. The rest of the yoga class went smoothly, but I kept a wary eye out for Billy, in case he decided to show up again.

After the morning yoga session, Greg and I decided to go get something to eat. I was famished. We went back to the restaurant. We walked into the crowded area, with its tables, made just for two people, spaced around the area, each with a tiny lamp in the center.

"Welcome," said the host. "This way please."

Greg and I followed the man. At first, I was curious as to why he didn't ask how many needed to be seated, before remembering that this was a couples retreat; and what couple wants a third party along?

Our waiter showed up. "Anything to drink?" he asked.

"Two coffees, please," I replied, before realizing that he was the same waiter who had served us last night. "Matherson," I read the nametag. "Is that a first or last name?"

"Oh, sorry," said our waiter. He recognized us. "It's you two."

"We can go, if it's a problem," said Greg, getting ready to stand up.

"No, it's quite all right," said Matherson. "Turns out,

you were telling the truth last night. It's my last name"—he pointed at his nametag—"I don't use my first name much."

"Oh? What is it?" I said, curious.

"Bernie."

"I can see why you don't like it," Greg said.

"It is not Bernie." Billy said, but only I heard him. "He doesn't look like a Bernie."

"Uh, I think we're ready to order," I said, trying to ignore Billy's comments.

Greg gave me a questioning look, but my glance told him that we needed to get rid of the waiter ASAP.

"Sure," Matherson held out his notepad.

"I mean, does he come across to you as a Bernie?" Billy continued.

"We'll both have waffles, with bacon," I told our waiter, "but I'd like mine with your peach sauce."

"Peach sauce?" exclaimed Billy. "That stuff will ruin your waffles."

I cringed, wishing that Billy would disappear. "Go away!" I hissed at him from the side of my mouth.

"What?" asked Matherson.

"Nothing," I said. "Can we get some cream with our coffee, too?"

"Sure," said our waiter.

"Fine," snapped Billy. "I can tell when I'm not wanted." He left.

"He was here again?" Greg asked after our waiter had gone.

"Yes," I replied, "but I think he left again."

"So, what do you want to do?"

"We need to find out if Chad really did kill Billy," I

said. "Maybe, when we're finished here, you can learn a little more about Chad, and I'll see about getting Billy to stop trying to exact revenge."

"Sounds good to me."

Our food arrived and we ate, not bothering to take our time as we both had things to do. Once done, we paid our check and left, running into Aimie and Patrick on the way out.

"Hey, you two," greeted Aimie. "Getting a bite to eat?"

"We just finished," I said, "but maybe later?"

"It's a date!" said Patrick.

"Oh, you guys"—Matherson, our waiter, ran up to us with the money we had used to pay out check—"because of last night's events, Emily has said that your meals here are free of charge. Sorry, I should have…"

He stopped speaking the moment he noticed Aimie and Patrick.

"Thanks," said Greg, taking the bills from Matherson's hand. "We really don't mind…"

"It's policy," said Matherson, with a robotic note to his voice, his eyes still focused on Aimie and Patrick. I thought I had seen recognition in them, but before I could say anything, Matherson left with a quick, "Have a nice day."

"What was that all about?" demanded Greg, confused. "He acted like he'd seen a ghost." He looked at me and I gave a quick shake of the head, answering his unspoken question. Billy was nowhere to be found.

"Probably nothing," said Patrick.

"We'll definitely catch up with you later," said Aimie, pushing Patrick along to a table.

We said our good-byes and left, walking out into the crisp air as it mingled with the warmth from a heating lamp.

"Okay, so we're agreed," I said. "You go find Chad and make sure Billy doesn't try something, and I'll see what I can find out around here."

"Just be careful," said Greg.

"You too."

Chapter 5

With a little bit of nosing around, I learned where Billy's apartment was. He lived on the resort in a small, one-bedroom place in the basement of the main building. Being the janitor, Emily had decided that it was best if he lived there so that if his services were needed, he would be available.

I glanced around as I approached the warped door of his apartment, making certain that no one saw me go in there. Thanks to all of the time I had spent with Tiny and his friends, I managed to jimmy the lock, which wasn't very secure to begin with, and slip inside, unnoticed. Darkness greeted me, except for a sliver of light that poked through the two foot, rectangular window. I felt for a light switch. The moment I had found it, I flipped it on.

I almost shrieked when I got a good look at Billy's apartment. What a mess! Empty bags of chips and cereal boxes lay strewn all over the floor. No matter where I stepped, my foot crunched candy wrappers and dried, hard candies that had melted into the stained carpet. My foot caught on a wire that had tangled on the thin fibers of the carpet, tripping me. I reached out, grabbing the sides of a chair, the smooth and gritty material making me cringe. I looked at the chair. Gum, burrowed into the threads of the fabric, dotted it in a multicolored coat of spit and stickiness. I lifted my hands off the chair, wiping them on my pants in a poor attempt to clean them.

Plastic cups rattled against one another as I crept through the room. Where would I start? I didn't know what I was searching for; I just knew that I had to find something that would tell me why Billy had been murdered. My hand brushed a pile of magazines, knocking them off of a nearby table, exposing a phone and answering machine. The number 4 flashed in red on the machine, indicating that there were messages.

I pressed the play button and listened to the four messages.

Message 1:

Hey, Billy! Where are you? I've been waiting here for 20 minutes.

Message 2:

Yes, Billy Randall, this is Tonia from the Heweitt

Creditors. I am calling to inform you that you are past due on the payments of your account. Please call me at 800-693-9100, extension 301. If you fail to contact me by the 5th of March, legal action will be taken.

Message 3:

Billy, I've been waiting here for over an hour for you to show up. If you're not here in five minutes, we're through!

Message 4:

Uh… wrong number.

I frowned. Nothing there for me to go on. I turned and meandered further into the room, knocking over a table in the process. It crashed to the floor and I cringed, hoping that no one had heard that. Something small and red caught my eye and I reached down and picked it up.

"Look at what you've done!" Billy yelled, popping into the room. "I had this place organized."

"Organized?" I replied. "You call this organized?"

"Well, what do you call it?" asked Billy.

"A disaster area." I kicked an empty beer can across the room to further illustrate my point.

"It is not! What are you doing here anyway?"

"Trying to figure out who murdered you and why."

"I already told you who did it." Billy's semi-transparent form turned red.

"But you said yourself that you never saw the person who struck you on the head," I said, trying to reason with him.

"But I know it was Chad!"

"How? Why?"

"Because.. because… I don't like him."

"Okay," I said.

"He has everything and…"

"That doesn't mean that he killed you," I interrupted him. "We need proof. Where were you when you died?"

"I was on the hiking trail that goes into town," said Billy.

"What were you doing there?"

"Does it matter?"

"Please, just answer the question."

"I was picking up garbage," said Billy. "People are such slobs sometimes!"

I glanced around the biohazard area I stood in, known as Billy's apartment. "Did you see anything?"

"It was dark. All I remember before I blacked out was seeing a pair of men's boots and Chad keeps a pair of boots in his locker."

"Only circumstantial evidence," I said. "I'm just saying," I added before Billy had a chance to lose his temper, "that it isn't enough to convict him."

I remembered the thumb-sized item I had picked up moments before and looked at it. The red object stared back at me; its brilliant exterior reflected the light above my head. Was this a jewel? It looked like a ruby, but was it real?

"Billy," I said, "what is this?"

"Just a paperweight," replied Billy as he scratched his partially exposed belly button.

"Are you sure?"

"Yeah. Why?"

I studied the red object more closely. It could have been made of glass, or a material that gave it its sheen, and be a paperweight, like Billy insisted, but there was the possibility that it was more than that. "It looks like an actual gem," I said. "A ruby."

"Nah, can't be," said Billy. "I found that while... um... while..."

"Yes?" I urged him.

"Well..."

"Where did you find it?"

"Chad's locker."

"What?" I almost dropped the item in my hand.

"That's how I know he's the one that murdered me!"

"Hold on," I said, trying to put the pieces together. "What were you doing going through Chad's locker?"

"Uh... I have this problem?"

"Are you a kleptomaniac?" I asked as I looked around at the radios, cell phones, gloves, scarves, shoes, purses, expensive looking pens, and e-readers.

"People just leave things lying around and I pick them up."

"You stole this."

"So?" said Billy.

"Look," I said, "is there a jeweler in town?"

"Yeah. Only one."

"I am going to get this looked at to make sure that it's

not a fake. Until then, I need you to promise me that you won't go after Chad?"

"No!" Billy disappeared.

I sighed in frustration and prayed that Greg would be able to protect Chad from Billy's antics. The last thing I needed was another murder happening at the hands of a vengeful ghost.

Chapter 6

I slipped out of the apartment, making certain to shut the light off and lock the door so that no one would know that someone had been in there. The empty hallway gave me an eerie feeling as I hurried down it amidst the dreary carpet and poor lighting. Emily must have poured most of her money into making the cabins and rooms luxurious, though I didn't understand why she couldn't have made the place where Billy lived a bit nicer, not that it would have mattered with his sloppiness.

Once outside, I hurried over to the trail that led into town, not wanting to waste any time in getting the red gem appraised. The bare trees and the gray snow made me think that I had entered a haunted forest. The frozen ground crunched beneath my boots. The trail had been cleared of snow, but pockets of ice still lined it, giving a loud—Crack!—with each step I took.

"What did you leave it in the room for?" demanded an irate voice, blocked by a few trees.

I stopped. Glancing around for the source, I soon realized that it wasn't talking to me, but came from the other side of a tree barrier. Ignoring it, I continued walking.

"Because you told me to, you ignoramus!" responded another voice.

I stopped again. Letting my curiosity get the better of me, I crept to the trees, and peeked through the split between them. On the other side were Morgan and Burt, arguing again.

"And you listened to me?"

"Oh, so I wasn't supposed to?" demanded Morgan, placing her pudgy hands on her hips.

Not wanting to get involved, I stepped away, but just as I moved my foot, a twig snapped; its sound echoed around me as I cringed, wishing I were invisible.

"Great," huffed Burt, "so now we have company."

"I'm sorry," I began, "I'll just go."

"No. No. Stay and watch the show," Burt said. "I'm sure you've heard most of it anyway. Morgan's voice is quite the spectacle."

"My voice?" snapped Morgan. "Have you listened to yourself lately? Your voice is so loud that it carries from here to Texas!"

"Oh, yeah? Well, I bet that the people of California are sick of hearing your nasally tone."

I started to walk away.

"Hey, where you going?" demanded Burt.

"Away from here," I said.

"See?" said Morgan, flipping her permed hair. "You scared her away."

"Well, she shouldn't be nosing around, spying on people."

"I wasn't…"

"Yeah, because she has nothing better to do than to listen to us."

"HEY!" I shouted, surprised by the forcefulness of my own voice. "Will you two shut up? All you do is argue!"

"Got a set of lungs on her, that one," commented Burt.

"I'll say," Morgan added in a complementary tone. "She got you to shut up."

"Not good enough. You're still talking."

"Stop it!" I shouted at them. "First off, I was not spying on you two; I was on my way to town, but your voices can be heard over a mile away. So, I decided to check it out, make sure nothing happened. You guys can stay here and fight all you want. I'm going to town."

"Now, hold on there," said Burt, "I didn't mean anything by what I said earlier, about you spying. We seem to attract attention everywhere we go."

I wonder why, I thought to myself.

"Stick around," said Morgan.

"Why do you two argue so much?" I asked, allowing my curiosity to lead me, once again.

"For fun," replied Morgan.

"Excuse me?" I said.

"Well, we've been married for a while now and sometimes you got to do something to liven things up," replied Burt. "About two years ago, Morgan and I were out and were having a real argument, and got kind of loud, but some people dubbed us the 'fighting couple' and I guess—"

"—it stuck," finished Morgan. "In the end, we couldn't remember what had started the fight, but we had so much fun arguing that we continue to do it."

"Seems like a strange pastime to me," I said.

"It does to most people," replied Morgan.

"We only argue in public," said Burt, "but when we're alone, we hardly fight at all. Besides, all this fake fighting gets off our chest whatever might have been bothering us all day."

"And we always make up in the end," added Morgan.

I just stared at them, still not believing that they argued on purpose for entertainment.

"Where were you headed, anyway?" asked Burt.

"To town," I said. "I was on my way to the local jeweler."

"Oh," said Morgan, "is that man of yours going to propose?"

"I…"

"Oh, we both noticed you two," Morgan interrupted me. "He's a keeper, that one."

My cheeks grew hot as I blushed, despite my best efforts not to. "He has been a bit secretive lately."

Morgan got one of those all-knowing smiles on her face, which made me blush even more.

"Yeah," said Burt, "in a few years, you'll look like us."

I must have gotten a panicked look on my face because Morgan swatted him, adding, "Now you're scaring her!"

"Going to the jeweler, you said?" asked Burt, checking his wristwatch.

"Yes, why?" I replied.

"Better hurry. He closes at five and it's nearly five now."

What! In talking to them, I had forgotten about the ruby in my pocket, which I had found in Billy's apartment. I said good-bye to Burt and Morgan, still perplexed about their idea of entertainment, and raced back to the cleared trail. My lungs burned as I ran, having not sprinted like this in a few years, while my fast breathing formed clouds of white vapor.

I made it to the small town with its locally owned shops lining the street and spotted the jewelry store right away. I dashed across the street and tugged at the door handle. Locked. I checked the hours posted on the glass door. Yep, the store closed at five and my watch said it was ten after.

Dismayed, I stared at the red paperweight, wishing that I had not stopped to talk to Burt and Morgan. How could I have allowed myself to get so distracted?

"Hey, Mel!"

I looked up. Approaching me from the other side of the street were Aimie and Patrick. I stuffed the ruby into my sweater pocket, hoping they didn't notice my quick movements, but they did.

"What's that?" asked Patrick, pointing at my pocket.

"Nothing," I replied, "just something I wanted to get looked at, but I was a little late in getting here."

"Well, maybe tomorrow then," said Patrick. "I'm told that this guy closes at five o'clock on the dot, not a minute sooner, or later."

"What are you two up to?" I asked.

"Just exploring the town," said Aimie. "I love visiting all of these little shops."

"And buying stuff," joked Patrick.

Aimie smacked him in response.

I smiled at their playfulness.

"Hey," said Aimie, "you owe us a lunch, or dinner, considering the time. Where's Greg?"

"Back at the resort. He doesn't like shopping much."

"That's a man thing," said Aimie, "but you should join us. We were just about to grab a bite at this place down the street here."

Not wanting to be rude and the fact, that my stomach growled just then, I agreed to join them.

We went to this Indian restaurant that Emily had told Greg and me about when we had first checked in. The owner, a jovial man who welcomed all who walked through the door with a smile and handshake, had emigrated from India about 30 years ago and established his restaurant as a way to introduce Americans to real, as he called it, Indian food. I felt a little odd being here by myself with Aimie and Patrick; the restaurant had been set up to accommodate couples, since it wasn't far from the resort.

"Three?" asked the owner as he greeted us, wearing an orange tuxedo, his coattails swaying with each movement.

"Yes," said Patrick.

Even though we were the only three person group there, he never said anything, but grabbed three menus and led us to a table. We took our seats and looked at the menu, more interested in what this place had to offer in the way of food, instead of talking. When the waiter arrived, we placed our orders. That was when the conversation started.

"They really decorated this place nice," said Patrick.

Aimie laughed. "Yeah, for couples."

She must have noticed me squirm because she added, "Oh, don't worry. We don't mind having you along. Besides, you did agree earlier to joining us sometime for a meal."

"How did you two meet?" I asked them.

"Work," said Aimie.

"We both are in the shipping business," added Patrick. "We transport goods from one place to another."

"Yeah, it was love at first sight," said Aimie.

"Oh, I don't know about that," Patrick joked, and received a playful smack in response.

"What about you and Greg?" Aimie asked.

"Well," I began, "believe it or not, he is my next door neighbor."

"What?" said Aimie in surprise.

"Yeah. We also attend the same college and that was where we had first met, with me dressed in a grungy pair of jeans and bed-hair."

Both Aimie and Patrick laughed, picturing my messy appearance.

I thought back to the day that Greg and I had met. It was the first day of classes, and my first class of the day, and I had arrived late, dressed in my usual attire of jeans and a t-shirt; and no, I hadn't bothered to brush out my hair. That was also when I had met Rachel, the first ghost

I had ever talked to, and whose murder I helped solve because she wouldn't leave me alone. Though, she still shows up from time to time.

"So what happened?" asked Aimie.

"Well," I replied, "Greg said hello to me, and we talked for a little bit, but I kind of brushed him off. Later that evening, he knocked on my door with a cake in his hand, but I was a little out of sorts and closed the door in his face.

"Really?' said Greg. "So, how'd you end up going out?"

"I have Rachel to thank for that." The words were out of my mouth before I had even realized that I had said them.

"Rachel?" asked Patrick.

"A friend," I replied. "She ensured that Greg and I met again, and we've been together ever since."

"So what do you do?" said Aimie.

"When I'm not in class at the college, I'm at work. I work at a little place called the Candle Shoppe, and the word shop is spelled s-h-o-p-p-e on the sign."

"How quaint," said Aimie. "So, no hobbies?"

"I don't have time for hobbies," I replied. I wasn't about to tell them that I speak to ghosts, or that they seek me out sometimes, asking for help. "Work and school—"

"—and Greg," Aimie finished for me.

"And Greg," I continued, "keep me busy. So, tell me more about your shipping business."

"Not much to tell," said Patrick. "Mostly traveling, and dealing with employees. Not long ago we had this one incident with someone who—"

"I don't think she wants to hear about that," Aimie cut him off.

"No, go on," I urged.

"Well, we caught him stealing," Patrick finished.

"Did you have him arrested?" I asked, intrigued.

"No," said Patrick. "I mean, the authorities were never able to catch him. He skipped town and could be anywhere."

"So what did you do?" I asked.

"Nothing," said Aimie. "We decided to just put it all behind us. Live and learn, you know."

Our food arrived and we stopped talking long enough to eat. While I reached for my fork, I tipped over my glass of water, knocking it off the table and spilling water everywhere. As I hurried to clean it up with a napkin, the red gem I had picked up from Billy's apartment fell out of my pocket. I scooped it up and shoved it back into my pocket, hoping no one had noticed, but I wasn't so lucky.

"What was that?" asked Patrick.

"Nothing," I replied.

"Really? Because…"

"It's nothing." My tone told him to drop it. The waiter showed up soon after with a towel and mopped up the water before replacing my drink. The rest of the meal was spent in minimal conversation.

"Thanks for supper," I said when we left the restaurant.

"It was our pleasure," said Patrick, as though the water incident had never happened, or my curt manner when the ruby had fallen out of my pocket. I didn't know if it was an actual ruby, or just a fake, but hoped that I would make it to the jeweler the next day.

"We should…" began Aimie, but I noticed Chad

across the street, walking past a set of tables with dinner-ware on display and a bag in his hands.

My phone rang. "Excuse me," I said as I answered it.

"Mel?" It was Greg. "I lost Chad. I'm sorry. I know I was supposed to keep an eye on him, but he started getting suspicious about me following him."

"I know where he is," I said.

"Really? Where?"

"Oh, about 50 yards away from me." I watched as he paused by a display window. I looked at Aimie and Patrick as they watched me. "I'm afraid I have to go, but I thank you for dinner. See you around?" I told them, placing my hand over the receiver of my phone.

"Sure. No problem," said Aimie, pulling Patrick away.

"Mel?" Greg said when I put the phone back to my ear.

"Don't worry about it," I told him. "I don't think…" My voice trailed off as I watched a dinner plate, from the display table, rise up into the air and follow after Chad. Oh no. Billy. "I got to go."

I hung up my phone and charged across the street towards Chad. The plate rose higher. I snatched it just before Billy could hit Chad with it, and placed it on another display table. Chad hadn't noticed anything.

Just then, a snow shovel that had been leaning against the wall, swooped into the air. I lunged for it, wrapping my fingers around the handle and dove behind a corner, just a Chad turned around, but he never saw me.

"Will you stop it?" I hissed at Billy, even though he remained invisible.

"No!" came his disembodied voice.

The shovel dropped in my hands and I knew that Billy had disappeared again. Peeking around the corner, I watched as an empty flower pot headed straight for Chad's head. Would this vendetta ever stop? I dropped the snow shovel and sprinted for the flower pot, stretching my hands out for it. I reached it just before Billy had a chance to hit Chad with it, but in my haste to stop him, I tripped and crashed into Chad, knocking us both to the pavement. The flower pot crashed on the ground, shattering, pieces spreading in every direction.

"What the—" shouted Chad as he smashed into the ground, with me landing beside him.

"Sorry! I... uh... I..." I sputtered, unsure of how to explain my actions.

"Are you okay?" asked Chad.

"Yeah, I..." I noticed that the ruby was not in my pocket. Frantic, I searched for it and found it on the sidewalk, with a black shoe next to it. I looked up into the very irate face of Matherson. I reached for the object, but he grabbed it before I could.

"Where did you get this?" he demanded.

"Give it back," I said, holding out my hand.

"Where did you get this?" Matherson said again, his tone suspicious.

"I found it. It's not even real," I replied.

"Is there a problem here?" asked Chad.

Matherson glanced across the street before putting the ruby in my hand, stepping closer so that he could speak to me without Chad overhearing him. "I wouldn't keep it, if I were you."

"What was that all about?" Chad asked after Matherson had left.

"I don't know," I said.

"And the thing in your hand?"

"Found it. It's pretty worthless."

"And the knocking me over?"

"An accident."

Chad gave me a disbelieving look, but what could I say? I couldn't tell him that a vengeful ghost was trying to exact some sort of revenge.

"You ruined everything!" Billy hissed into my ear.

I ignored him. Now was not the time to talk to a ghost.

"Fine! Don't listen to me." Billy vanished, though I had a feeling that he wouldn't be gone for long.

"What brings you to town?" I asked Chad.

"Emily has a bit of a cold and sent me here to the 24 hour pharmacy for some cough medicine." Chad held up the bag. "I was on my way back."

"Really? So was I."

"I'll walk with you then."

Fine with me. At least, then, I could make sure that Billy didn't try anything. Once on the trail that led back to Emily's, I shivered, wishing that I had remembered to wear something better suited for a hike in the cold. Chad gave me his coat.

"Won't you get cold?" I asked him.

"No, the cold doesn't bother me that much," he said. "Where's your boyfriend? I thought you two would be together."

"I wanted to do a little shopping," I told him, maintaining the story I had told Aimie and Patrick, "and he isn't that big on it."

"Oh."

"Is something bothering you?"

"What was all of that back there?"

"Nothing," I said, "I noticed the flower pot hanging from above about to fall on you and thought I would try to catch it before it did. Guess I wasn't so graceful."

"And the incident in your cabin, when you had me look at the fridge even though nothing was wrong with it."

"Greg insisted that it wasn't working properly."

"And then the incident this morning with the tree branch?"

I didn't answer right away. How could I? What would I say? Hello, Chad. This Billy, who worked as a janitor, and whose dead body turned up in my room, his ghost is haunting you, convinced that you killed him. I don't think that would go over too well.

"You don't have a crush on me, do you?"

"No!" That came out ruder than I had meant it to.

"It's happened before. One woman came here with her boyfriend and started hitting on me. Her boyfriend was not pleased and there was a bit of a heated confrontation between us."

"Heated confrontation?"

"A few punches were thrown. That was it."

"It's not like that," I assured him.

"Then why is it your boyfriend has been following me around all day; and when I go into town, I run into you?"

Before I could think of an excuse, a snowball crashed

into Chad from behind and I found myself glad that Billy had shown up. "Take that you murdering jerk!"

Chad turned around, staring at the wooded scenery behind us and I knew that he had heard Billy's outburst, even if he didn't see him. "What was that?"

"Probably just some kids," I said.

"Calling me a murdering jerk?"

"You know how they are."

I motioned for Billy to go away, while trying to make sure that Chad didn't notice.

"Well, he is!" shouted Billy, throwing another snowball at Chad before disappearing.

Chad just stood there, confused as to how a snowball had managed to throw itself.

"Let's just go," I said, pulling him along. Please, do not ask me what had just happened, I thought to myself.

The rest of our walk was done in silence. I knew that Billy's antics had confused Chad. It's not every day you see something move of its own accord. When we arrived back at the resort, red and blue flashing lights greeted us. Confused, we both headed for them, while I prayed that no one else turned up dead, and that Billy hadn't decided to do something stupid just to get his revenge.

"Mel!" Greg ran up to us.

"Greg, what's—"

"They're looking for him!" Greg pointed at Chad, yanking me away from him.

"What? Why?" I said, still confused as to what was happening.

"Mr. Seagel?" said an officer, approaching Chad.

"Yes," answered Chad.

"I am placing you under arrest for the murder of Billy Sunders."

"What?" screamed Chad. "I didn't do anything!"

The officer turned Chad around, and placed his arms behind his back before handcuffing him.

"Yeah!" said Billy, but only I heard him. "Take that, you murderer!" He threw another snowball at Chad.

I glared at Billy.

"What?" he said to me, noticing my disapproving look. "I didn't do it."

"You threw the snowball."

"No, I mean the murder weapon."

"What?"

"Yeah," said Billy, "they found the thing used to knock me on the head in Chad's locker. Emily had agreed to a search."

Billy left to continue taunting Chad, much to the confusion of the officers around us.

"I don't get it." I said. "Why stay here, if he killed Billy?"

"Maybe he thought that running would make him look guilty," said Greg. "The murder weapon was found in his locker."

"Why did the police wait so long to search through the lockers?"

"The detective on the case wanted a warrant, but I overheard Emily say that she would have agreed to it no matter what. She wants this whole thing over with."

I couldn't blame her on that one.

"Maybe we ought to leave," I heard one guy say to

his girlfriend. "I don't think this place is safe. Hiring a murderer and all."

Emily stood outside, watching the proceedings and I could tell she had overheard what that man had said as a panicked look crossed her face and she chewed her nails. The poor woman. I knew that she was seeing the dismal future of her business right then.

I hated to say it, but I had to agree with Greg; it looked like Chad had actually done it. As I listened in on the conversations around me from the other guests, I learned that it was a small club that had been used to strike Billy over the head. It still had his blood on it when they found it buried in Chad's locker, and Chad had been keeping an eye on Greg and me ever since Billy's corpse turned up in our cabin. It all fit.

"Come on," said Greg, taking Chad's jacket from around my shoulders and placing his own on them, "let's go."

"I guess I owe Billy an apology," I said. "He was right."

"Hey!" Aimie ran up to us. "Can you believe it? And to think that you were alone with him in the woods all of that time."

That just made me feel worse.

"Emily is having a gathering by the fireplace in the lounge," Aimie continued. "There will be free drinks and everything. We should go."

"I really don't…"

"It probably wouldn't hurt," interrupted Greg. "She might have something important to say."

"Sure," I said. "I just need to drop something off in our room first. Meet you two there?"

"Sure. I'll just text Patrick, so he knows where I am."

I stopped off at the honeymoon cabin that Emily had put Greg and me in after our original accommodations had been turned into a crime scene. Once inside, I switched out Greg's jacket for my own, but kept his so that I could give it back to him once I got to the lounge, and placed the red paperweight, as Billy called it, in a dresser drawer. I still wanted to get it checked out by a jeweler. It looked like a real gemstone, but there are so many realistic fakes that I wanted to be sure.

Once I had what I needed, I turned off the lights and locked the door.

Chapter 7

The raucous crowd filling the lodge deafened my ears when I entered through its double glass, and timber wood doors. People clumped together in small groups, talking so loud that their voices echoed all around me as I navigated my way to where Greg and Aimie waited for me.

"Where's Patrick?" I asked Aimie.

"He'll be along," she replied. "Probably lost in this crowd."

I glanced around and laughed. The lodge was packed.

"Attention! Attention!" Emily had set up the karaoke machine and used its microphone so that she could speak over the crowd. "Please, may I have your attention."

The crowd settled some, but murmurs still rumbled through it.

"I know that the last couple of days have been a bit of an upset," said Emily.

"A bit?" shouted one angry voice. "A murder took place right here!"

"Yeah," said another within the crowd, "and it turns out that the murderer was one of your employees."

"Please! Please!" Emily pleaded. "In an effort to compensate you for the interruption of your stay here, I am handing out, by the doors there, vouchers for a three night stay, all expenses paid. Good until the end of the year."

Angry murmurs filled the room as some thought that Emily was trying to bribe them into not suing her. I looked at the poor woman in her frazzled state. Her face had gone ashen and her eyes showed nothing but panic. I knew that the last thing she wanted was a lawsuit and didn't blame her in trying to bribe the patrons here with a free, three night stay. How was she to know that Chad would murder someone?

"Hey! What did I miss?" asked Patrick as he showed up, wrapping his arms around Aimie.

"Not much," said Aimie. "Emily has offered vouchers for a free three nights here, but some of these folks don't seem happy about it."

"How could you let someone like that work here?" demanded a guy standing next to us with his wife. A few others voiced the same sentiment.

"Please," said Emily, "I didn't—"

"Don't you do background checks on your employees!" shouted another.

"Hey, lay off her!" yelled Patrick, losing his temper. "It's not her fault that some nut job decided to off someone."

"Who are you?"

"Doesn't matter! My girlfriend and I, we'll take one of those vouchers."

Aimie grinned and kissed Patrick. "You're the best," she whispered in his ear.

"We'll take some too," said Greg, raising his hand.

With the two of them hurrying to Emily's defense, the crowd settled down. Some just left, saying that they had had enough and were' leaving before anyone else turned up dead. Others either took a voucher, or went back to their rooms.

"Do you two want a night cap?" asked Patrick of Greg and I. "There is a bar in the restaurant here and it's pretty good."

I yawned. "Sorry," I apologized, "I'm beat. I think I'd rather just go to bed."

"Oh, honey," said Aimie, "no problem. Night then."

Greg took my hand and we walked back to our cabin. I hoped that Emily's business would be able to get through this unscathed. The closer we got to the door of the honeymoon cabin, the more I thought about snuggling into bed with the covers pulled up to my chin. I should have known that I would never be allowed to go to bed.

Greg unlocked the door and held it open for me. The moment I turned on the light, I froze. Our cabin had been ransacked. The cushions from the couch lay in the kitchenette area, while the plants had been overturned, but that wasn't what drew my attention. Instead, my eyes focused on the pair of black-soled feet poking out from behind the sofa. I pointed them out to Greg.

He pushed me back outside and crept over to the shoes, stopping the moment he was two feet from them. "Better call the cops," he said. "This man is dead."

I hurried over to Greg's side and looked down. Matherson, our waiter from this morning and last night, lay dead on the carpet.

"Something tells me that Chad might not have murdered me after all," said Billy, appearing beside me.

I ran to the bedroom. It was in the same disarray as the rest of the cabin with the covers of the bed torn off and tossed aside; our pillows had been ripped out of their cases. I couldn't believe what I saw. Why would anyone want to search our cabin?

The top drawer on the dresser was ajar. I yanked it open and tore through it, knowing what I would find. The ruby I had discovered in Billy's apartment was gone.

Chapter 8

Within 10 minutes of placing the call, the police arrived, once again, to Emily's special getaway spot for couples. I watched as the poor woman stood on the sidelines, chewing all of her nails, no doubt worrying about how this would affect her business. This was the second dead body to show up this weekend on her property.

"Did you know this man?" asked an officer as an EMT crew carted out the corpse in a black bag.

"No," both Greg and I replied.

"Do you know why he was in your room?"

"No," I said.

"Have you seen him before?" the officer continued his questions.

"He was our waiter this morning," said Greg.

"But you said that you didn't know him," the officer challenged.

"Oh, give me a break," snapped Billy, beside me. "Just because you speak to someone, doesn't mean that you know them."

"Look," I said, growing irritated, "he was our waiter when we ate at the restaurant last night and this morning at breakfast, but we had never met him until then, nor have we seen him since."

"A witness said that he saw you and the victim in town earlier this afternoon, talking to the suspect we arrested earlier today," the officer continued.

I had forgotten about that. "I was in town today and ran into him. I said, 'Excuse me.' And that was it. The exchange only lasted about two minutes."

"Coincidental," said the officer.

"If you are trying to imply," Greg broke in, "that she had something to do with this man's death, you are mistaken. She was with me in the lounge, surrounded by other people, the entire time."

"Excuse me," a detective on the case interrupted us and the officer left. "Though I must say that this is highly unusual, the coroner has declared that the man died sometime during the gathering in the lounge. As your boyfriend, and a few others have vouched for your whereabouts, you are free to go, for the moment."

Greg tried to lead me away, but the detective stopped us. "One other thing. I called the local police department where you live and spoke to a Detective Shorts. He has warned me that you have a tendency to… poke around. I told him that you had been remarkably quiet around here. You haven't found anything you wish to tell me about, have you?"

I had considered telling him about the possible ruby I had discovered in Billy's apartment, but thought better of it. I had acquired it by breaking and entering, and it also went missing before I had a chance to find out if it was real or not. "No."

"He said that you would say that. Detective Shorts also said that if you are investigating another murder on your own, you should stop. Now, are you certain there is nothing else you wish to tell me?"

Both Greg and I remained silent.

"Very well," said the detective, "you may go."

Greg and I walked away and were soon accosted by a frantic Emily.

"Oh, my goodness!" she burst out. "I can't even begin to apologize for all of this. Two murdered people turning up in your cabin! You will have a new room—yes, that's what I'll do."

"We're fine," I said. "We'll stay in the cabin after the police are finished."

"No!" shouted Emily. "You can't! You must be traumatized."

"It's not the first time I've seen a dead body," I said. That was true enough. I had run into a lot of them over the past three years. It didn't even phase me anymore.

"It's good of you to be brave, dear," said Emily, "but you don't need to cheer me up."

"Why don't you sit down?" Greg helped Emily to

a lounge chair, concerned, like I was, that her fretting might cause her to have a stroke. I couldn't blame her worrying. I knew that as she watched guests stroll by, and listened to some of their hushed whispers, that she saw her business going down the drain; and all of it after investing so much money into renovating it.

"I'll be fine," Emily said, waving a hand.

After the police had left, Greg and I retrieved our belongings, being moved, once again, to another room. Emily insisted, and there was no turning her down.

"So what were they looking for?" asked Greg.

"A ruby I found."

"A what?"

"Well, I don't know if it was a real ruby, or a very convincing fake. I tried taking it to the local jeweler in town, but got there after he had closed. Somehow, somebody knew I had it."

"So where is it?"

"Gone," I said. "Whoever searched this place, found it."

"Could that be why Matherson was here?"

"I don't know."

Greg pulled out his phone.

"What are you doing?" I asked.

"I know someone who can find out," he replied, pulling out his phone. "Jack," he said after his call connected, "I need some information."

I could just image Jack's groan on the other end.

"Look, I need a favor," said Greg. "Someone broke into our cabin here and we need to know why... No, I don't know who... Just look up someone named Matherson, who lives and works in this area. I don't know his real name. And call me back." He hung up.

"He'll call back later," Greg told me.

I noticed him slip something into his pocket, acting secretive like he did when we had first arrived.

"What's that?" I asked.

"Nothing," Greg replied.

"What is in your pocket?" I demanded.

"Quoting movies now?" teased Greg.

"You are acting a little weird."

"Look…"

A knock stopped him. We grabbed our bags and trooped down to the door where Emily stood, ready to take us to our new room. We followed her outside into the night air as she waddled before us, fretting to herself about what a tragedy this was. Despite our reassurances that we were fine, Emily continued to apologize for everything that had happened.

She took us into the main building and up a flight of steps to the second floor. Its cozy and romantic atmosphere would make you think that nothing was wrong. We followed her halfway down the corridor where she stopped before a wood door with the number 25 on it.

Emily swiped the keycard, allowing the lock to click as it opened, before handing it to Greg. "I know this isn't one of our cabins, but I haven't any more vacant ones. Do make yourselves at home and if you need anything, food, extra blankets, please, don't hesitate to let me know."

"We'll be fine. Thanks," said Greg.

Emily smiled at his efforts to make her feel better and rushed off, murmuring, "Oh, dear. Oh, dear."

"Now," I said, placing my suitcase on the bed, "will you tell me what you are hiding in your pocket?"

"I'm not…" His phone rang.

I frowned as he answered it, knowing that I would never receive an answer to my question.

"Jack?" Greg answered, putting his phone on speaker.

"You know, getting involved in a murder is hardly romantic," said Jack.

"What did you find out?" Greg asked, ignoring Jack's comment.

"Well, it took some digging, but not much," said Jack. "Matherson is really John Mathers. The fingerprint analysis that the local PD ran through matched the same fingerprints for a man named John Mathers who is wanted in connection with a robbery. He was a pretty good thief. Broke into some rich guy's penthouse and stole what is known as the Red Heart. It's a ruby about the size of your thumb."

"That thief!" came a harsh voice. I looked behind me and found Billy, who had decided to turn up out of nowhere. "That's why I took that ruby from him. The thief."

"You told me it was a paperweight," I said to him.

"Yeah, well… that was a cover," said Billy.

"You also told me that you took it from Chad."

"I… kind of lied," said Billy.

"What's going on?" asked Jack. "Who's that with you?"

"Just Mel," said Greg. "Will you tell him to keep it down?" Greg hissed at me.

"Hey, I don't appreciate—"

"Billy!" I stopped him.

"Fine." Billy folded his arms. "Ungrateful."

"So, this Matherson guy is really John Mathers?" asked Greg.

"According to the fingerprint analysis," replied Jack. "He disappeared two years ago, changed his name, got some plastic surgery done to change his face, and was never seen again until he turned up dead at the same place you two are supposed to be having a romantic, Valentine's Day getaway."

"Is there anything else?" asked Greg.

"Well, it's believed that he had two accomplices, but the police couldn't prove anything and had no leads to go on. The New York police seemed surprised to find him turn up there."

"Okay. Thanks, Jack." Greg ended the call.

"Do you think his two accomplices caught up with him?" I asked.

"Sounds like it," said Greg.

"We need to find that ruby," I said.

"You lost it!" shouted Billy, causing Greg to jump. He could hear Billy, but couldn't see him.

"You saw our place and what a mess it was. Someone had clearly searched it," I replied.

"HMMPPH!" Billy crossed his arms. "First you refuse to believe that Chad had killed me."

"Which I seem to be right about," I said.

"And then," continued Billy, ignoring my statement, "you break into my apartment and steal my ruby."

"Which you had insisted was a paperweight and it was buried under cheese wrappers," I said.

"We need to find that ruby," said Greg. Whoever killed Matherson, must have known he had had it at one time, before learning that you had somehow acquired it. But, if Billy had stolen it from Matherson, how did he know to search our place?"

"I ran into Matherson while in town and he saw me with it. Seemed rather upset about it, but Chad was also there and told him to leave."

"Whoever has it is the real murderer!" blurted out Billy; his beer belly jiggled as he jumped up and down.

"I hate to say it, Greg," I said, "but I think Billy is correct; and we need to search the other rooms to find out who does have the ruby."

"But these locks are different from your normal ones that take a key," said Greg. "We need the pass key to get in."

I slumped on the bed. He was right. Without a pass-key, there was no way we could get into the other rooms. Also, how were we to make sure that no one was in there? Billy. I turned and looked at him.

"Why are you looking at me like that?" he asked.

"You can help us," I told him.

"No!" Billy folded his arms, his gut poking out from underneath his shirt. "I'm not gonna."

"But it will mean finding the real person who killed you," I said. "Even you admitted that it couldn't have been Chad."

Billy opened his mouth and closed it again, incensed that I had reminded him of something he had said earlier.

"And you can also help by letting us know if the rooms are empty or not," I told him.

"I don't know if I should," snapped Billy. "You haven't been very nice to me."

I clamped my mouth shut in an effort to avoid yelling at him. He's the one who kept trying to hit Chad over the head with something in some misguided attempt to seek justice. "I'm sorry," I mumbled.

"What?" said Billy, facing me. "I didn't hear you."

"I'm sorry," I said aloud.

"Apology accepted," said Billy. He disappeared.

"So," said Greg, "will he help us?"

"I think so."

Pop! Billy appeared beside me with the passkey, which I'm sure Emily was racking her brains trying to figure out where it had disappeared to. "Let's go," said Billy, waving the passkey in front of me.

"Uh, Billy, maybe I should take that." I reached for the key.

"Why?"

"I don't think many people will take it too well if they see that thing floating by itself."

"Oh." He handed me the key.

"But, thank you," I said to him and his face brightened.

We all slipped out of the room—Billy remained invisible—and went to the first two doors next to ours.

"We should split up," said Greg. "We can search faster. Just keep your phone on."

"Okay," I agreed.

I wasn't sure how many rooms would be empty, since

it was late, but it seemed that most people chose to stay up, visiting the lounge or the patio area, unable to sleep after the night's events.

Billy poked his head through a door. "No one."

I swiped the passkey, unlocking the door, and Greg went inside. "Don't take too long," I told him.

He kissed me, promising that he would be careful.

Billy poked his head into the next room. "Clear."

Once again, I swiped the passkey and went inside. Nothing unusual stood out to me as I looked at the organized room with the open suitcase in the corner, a few shirts poking out of it. That was the first place I searched, but all I found were socks, underwear, and a few phone chargers. The nightstand only obtained a Bible and some notepads with a pen that didn't work. There was nothing concealed under the mattress. Satisfied that there was nothing of interest here, I left and found Greg and Billy waiting for me to open the next door.

Once Billy checked to make sure it was empty, I opened the door and Greg went in. Billy beat me to the next one and started jumping up and down in front of it. "It's empty!" he exclaimed.

Smiling at how much of a thrill he was getting out of all of this, I opened the door and went in. What a mess! It almost put Billy's apartment to shame. Towels were strewn all over the bathroom floor, and the bed had not been made at all; or if had, the residents had messed it up again. Jeans, sweaters, and a frilly top were anywhere, but in the dresser or closet.

My foot snagged on something. Looking down to

see what I had gotten tangled up in, I realized that my foot had found a yellow thong which had, somehow, gotten tangled up in the bed post and a chair leg, forming a snare, perfect for tripping someone. I freed my foot, not wanting to know what went on in this room. Unfortunately, I was about to find out.

Laughter spilled down the hallway, coming closer to the door. Realizing I was about to get caught, I snuck into the only hiding place I could find: the closet. I had shut the door to it just as a man and a woman ran in, their lips locked and their hands working at a furious pace to remove the other's clothing. In an effort to remain hidden, I scrunched against the wall, but the heel of my boot scrapped against the bottom edge of the ironing board that was in there.

"What was that?" asked one of them.

"Nothing," said the other.

I peeked through the small opening of the door. They had moved closer to the bed, but there was no way I could make a mad dash to the door without being seen. My phone buzzed. Greg had sent me a text.

Where are you?

Trapped in a closet, I texted back. Help!

You okay? came another text.

About to get a peep show. Get me out of here! I replied.

A knock sounded at the door.

"Who was that?" asked the woman, pulling up her bra.

The man went and opened the door, but no one was there, telling me exactly who had knocked on it. He shut the door and went back to his girlfriend. "It was no one."

A loud bang rattled the door; so loud, that it made me jump, almost giving away my position.

Annoyed, the man went back to the door and yanked it open. "Hey, why don't you…" He stopped speaking when he realized that no one was there.

"Uh, honey," said the woman, "what's going on?"

"There's no one there."

Before the man could go back to his girlfriend, Billy's obnoxious voice filled the room. "GET OUT OF HERE YOU IDIOTS!"

There was no telling them twice. Each snatched their clothing and bolted through the door, not caring if they were half-naked. I rubbed my forehead. On the one hand, I had just been saved from being discovered in the closet of someone else's room; on the other hand, a rumor would now spring up about how Emily's place was haunted. Not sure if such a thing would be good for business: two murders and now a ghost screaming at guests.

I crawled out of the closet. "Thanks," I said to Billy. I wasn't about to scold him for what he did, as he did save my bacon. "Let's get out of here before they come back."

"Something tells me they won't," said Billy.

Probably not, I thought to myself, I know I wouldn't.

Greg came up to me the moment I left the room. "You okay?"

"Fine," I said. "What happened?"

"I asked Billy if he would help you," said Greg. "I didn't know if he was close enough to hear me, but thought it was worth a shot."

"That was kind of fun," said Billy to me. "Can I do it again?"

"No," I said to Billy, and then mimed to Greg that I was talking to the ghost, not him.

"Why is it he acts like I'm not around?" said Billy, pointing at Greg.

"Because he doesn't know you're here," I replied. "You could make yourself visible."

"Oh."

We searched the remaining rooms, but found no sign of the ruby, or anything that would tie someone to Billy's, or Matherson's, murder. Exhausted, Greg and I decided to just go to bed, since most of the guests had trickled up the stairs, deciding to do the same thing.

I didn't know what else to do and hoped that the next morning would bring new insight into the case.

Chapter 9

Two in the morning. No matter how much I tried, I was not able to get to sleep. I managed about two hours, but now lay wide awake, staring at the dimpled ceiling, wondering if I would ever get any sleep. I looked at the clock. It was now two minutes past.

Unable to get back to sleep, I sat up and rubbed my face, while listening to Greg's even breathing as he slept. A closing door caught my attention. It wasn't the fact that the door had closed that alerted me to its presence, but the fact that the one closing it had tried to do so in a manner that would not attract anyone's notice. Most people just allowed their doors to slam shut, but this person was trying to not make any noise, except that I heard the distinct click of the latch.

Curious as to who would be going out at this hour, I got out of bed—Greg shifted, but never opened his eyes—and went to the door, opening it a crack to peek out. All I saw was the back of a woman in a white sweatshirt and knit hat pulled past the tips of her ears. Where could she be going? The kitchen in the resort and the restaurant were closed. Most of the staff had gone home, except for the person who manned the front desk, meaning that the massage parlor, sauna, and lounge were also shut up tight. Everything in town would be closed as well.

Another scuffle sounded down the hall, forcing the woman to pause before hurrying down the steps, again trying to make no noise. Letting my curiosity dictate my movements, I slipped on my boots and coat, snatched my keycard, and left the room. I tiptoed down the hall, grateful that there was a rug to muffle the sounds of my feet.

I reached the edge of the stairs and looked down just in time to see a speck of white disappear. Not wanting to lose her, I hurried down the stairs and out the door, diving behind a pillar to avoid detection. The woman had paused to text someone. I craned my neck for a better look. If only I could see her face. My foot slipped and plopped on the solid ground, making a sudden noise that echoed. The woman whipped around just as I managed to hide. I cursed at my lack of stealth, but it had allowed me see the woman's face: Aimie.

What was she doing? And where was Patrick? Aimie looked at her phone, reading another text and replied, before taking off down the walk and heading for the hiking trail that led to the local town. I followed. I couldn't think of a reason for her to be out here in the middle of the night.

I kept my distance as I walked after her. She never looked behind. Her phone beeped and she looked at it. A frown formed on her face. Something had upset her. She fired off another text and rammed her phone into her pocket, continuing her trek through the small wooded area.

I maintained my pace and distance from her. She wasn't acting like the Aimie I had spoken with hours earlier. The farther away we got from the resort, the more I wished that I had remembered to wake Greg. I reached in my coat pocket for my phone. Nothing. In my haste, I had forgotten to grab it.

"Billy," I whispered, not sure if he would show up when called, or if he could even hear me. "Billy?"

No response. I hadn't expected there to be any, but it was worth a try. The clear, moonless night made it difficult for me to keep Aimie within sight, despite the white jacket she wore. I had thought about turning around and going back, torn between learning what Aimie was up to and wanting to get back to Greg. I settled on returning to the resort. My curiosity would have to wait for another time.

Just as I turned around, my foot found a patch of ice and I slipped, landing hard on the ground. My fall had alerted Aimie to my presence. She whirled around, holding something in her gloved hand, and yelled, "Who's there?"

I didn't say anything.

"I know you're there! Come closer."

Unable to pretend that I wasn't sitting on my bruised bottom in the middle of snow and ice, I stood up and walked towards Aimie.

"Mel?" she said, confused. "What are you doing here?"

"I… I heard you leave your room."

"And you followed me?"

"It seemed odd that you would be sneaking out in the middle of the night, alone." I spotted the gun in her hand and finally put it together. All of her friendliness and open invitations were just an act. "Why did you kill Billy?" I asked her.

"Billy?"

"The janitor?"

Aimie seemed shocked that I even knew. "How did you know?"

"You just told me," I replied.

"I never meant… he just… he caught Patrick and I snooping through the lockers. I grabbed the first thing I could find and hit him over the head. I only meant to knock him out. He wasn't supposed to die!"

"And Matherson? Were you and Patrick his accomplices during that New York heist when the ruby went missing?"

"How did you… she began. "I should have known. Patrick said he saw you snooping around."

"Why kill him, Aimie?"

"Patrick said it was an accident," replied Aimie. Her phone beeped, but she ignored it. "Matherson recognized us the moment we ran into you at the restaurant. We had helped him steal that ruby and he had promised to split the profits from selling it with us, but then he disappeared with it. We have spent the last two years trying to track him down. During our search, we learned that he had changed his face and spent his days working at some getaway place on the east coast. So, Patrick and I have been visiting every resort in an effort to find him."

"Why kill him?" I asked, trying to buy time while I thought of a way out of this situation.

"He wasn't supposed to! We were searching the lockers for a reason, but learned that you had somehow ended up with the ruby. Patrick saw it in your pocket when we went to dinner. We thought he could slip into your cabin and get it before anyone noticed, but Matherson must have had the same idea. He surprised Patrick and a fight ensued. No one was supposed to die! Patrick panicked."

"And hiding the murder weapon in Chad's locker?"

"With the cops coming around, and people on edge because of a murder, we thought it best to try and throw the suspicion on someone else. Patrick wiped my prints off of the weapon and placed it in a locker; he didn't know whose."

"Aimie, where's Patrick?"

"Waiting for me in town." Her phone beeped again. "I liked you, Mel"—she aimed the gun at me—"I really did."

"You could just let me go," I said.

"You'll tell the cops."

"I don't have my phone with me," I said. "By the time I make it back to the main building and phone the police, you and Patrick could be halfway to Canada."

I could tell that Aimie considered what I had said. She didn't want to shoot me, but she also didn't want to go to prison. I took a step back. Her grip on the weapon tightened.

"Mel, don't."

"Just let me go," I said.

"Don't make me…"

At that moment, a low-hanging branch pulled back, on its own, and snapped, striking Aimie in the head. Seizing the opportunity, I tackled her, knocking the gun out of her hands. We rolled across the snow-encrusted ground, each trying to get the upper hand. The gun didn't lie far. Together, we bolted for it, but before Aimie got to her knees, something hit her on the head, knocking her out.

Billy materialized the moment Aimie dropped to the ground. "I did it! I got my revenge!"

"Uh… thanks, Billy," I said, while checking to make certain that Aimie wasn't injured. She was just unconscious.

"Do you think you could keep an eye on her, while I go call the police?" I asked him.

"No problem. She won't get away from me." Billy crossed his arms in a triumphant stance, making me laugh.

I jumped to my feet and ran back to the resort, not caring how tired my legs were. Once I reached it, I burst into the main building and rushed the front desk. "I need a phone!"

The lady there gave me a strange look.

"Now!"

She handed me the desk phone and I dialed 911. Once someone answered, I explained everything in a rush and hung up.

"Mel!" Greg ran towards me in his pajamas and un-tied shoes. "Where've you…"

"It was Aimie and Patrick," I said, interrupting him. "They killed Billy and Matherson. Aimie is out there, now, unconscious."

Sirens wailed outside. "How did they get here so fast?"

"I woke up and you were missing," Greg answered. "When I noticed your coat missing as well, but your phone was still on the night stand, I called the police, afraid that you were in trouble."

When the police pulled up, I took them to where I had left Aimie. She was still lying in the snow uncon-scious with a triumphant Billy lording over her, not that anyone, but me, saw him.

"I did good, didn't I?" Billy asked in excitement, pleased that he had stopped Aimie.

"Yes," I whispered, hoping no one, but Billy, heard me, "you did well."

"I knew it was her and that twitchy boyfriend of hers."

I glared at him. Only hours before, he had been cer-tain that it was Chad who had killed him.

Aimie was taken into custody, but they never found Patrick. Greg must have noticed my frustration because he said to me, "Don't worry. They'll get him."

Once the detectives had finished questioning us, and the other guests went back inside, having gotten bored from watching another incident with the police, Greg and I went back to our room, where I finally fell asleep.

Chapter 10

When I awoke the next morning, the entire place was abuzz over last night's events. Greg and I had decided to check out. We had had enough of this romantic getaway, which had turned out to be anything, but romantic. As I folded one of Greg's pairs of jeans, a small, velvet box fell out of the pocket; the same box that I had noticed him trying to hide from me earlier. I picked it up.

"Greg," I said.

He poked his half-shaven face out of the bathroom.

"What is this?" I held up the tiny box.

"Um…"

"You've been hiding this from me all weekend."

"I, uh…"

"What is it?" I asked.

He put his razor down and took the box from me. "I had hoped to make this a very special weekend."

"But I messed it up."

"No! Things have not gone as planned, but... I don't know why spirits seek you out, but it proves what I've always known: that you are a very special person." Greg opened the box, revealing a small, diamond ring. "I had hoped to give this to you under better circumstances. Will you..."

"Yes!" I jumped at him, embracing him in a giant hug and giving him a long kiss.

"Well, if you ask me, it's about time," said Billy, appearing before us. He must have decided to allow Greg to see him, since Greg jumped back in surprise.

"Billy," I said, "what are you doing here?"

"I wanted to apologize," replied Billy, "for ruining your weekend."

"It's fine," I told him.

"You should know that they caught Patrick," said Billy. "I guess when Aimie didn't show up, he decided to turn himself in."

"And Chad?"

"He's been released."

I gave him a look.

"And I promise not to hurt him."

"So, what are your plans now?" I asked.

"I think I will stick around. This place needs a resident ghost," Billy replied.

"You could move on, you know."

"Yeah, but Rachel says..."

"You've seen Rachel!" both Greg and I said together. "When?" I demanded.

Billy didn't answer me. "I've got to go. Bye!"

I watched as he vanished in front of me, wanting to know what Rachel was up to. Knowing that she could be very unpredictable, I finished packing. In an hour, we left our room and trooped down to the front desk to check out, running into Morgan and Burt.

"Oh, I knew you two would be leaving engaged," said Morgan, noticing the ring on my finger.

I blushed a little at her outburst.

"He proposed!" Rachel burst into the hallway, fully visible to everyone, and snatched my hand, jumping up and down, while twisting me in circles. "I knew he would. I mean, you guys are the perfect couple, aside from the whole ghost and solving a murder thing. Oh, but you're engaged!"

She stopped. Her eyes moved from Burt to Morgan and back to Burt, realizing that they actually saw her. With an embarrassed smile she vanished.

Before I could say anything, both Burt and Morgan ran down the hallway to get away from us. "I think we better leave," I said to Greg.

And that's exactly what we did. He checked us out and I put our bags in the trunk of the car, ready to get on the road with my new fiancé. I just hoped that Rachel hadn't planned some big surprise party back home.

Get book 10 in the series

Double, Double, Nothing But Trouble

About the Author

Ms. McNulty began writing short stories at an early age. That passion continued through college until she published her first book: Legends Lost: Amborese under the pen name of Nova Rose. Since then, she has gone on to publish a mystery series, children's books, and even a dystopian series.

Ms. McNulty currently lives in West Virginia, where she enjoys hiking, being outside, crocheting, or simply sitting around and doing nothing. She continues writing and is busy working on the next book in her Mellow Summers Series as well as her science fiction adventure series: Solaris.

More by Janet McNulty

The Mellow Summers Series

Sugar And Spice And Not So Nice
Frogs, Snails, And A Lot Of Wails
An Apple A Day Keeps Murder Away
Three Little Ghosts
Oh Holy Ghost
Where Trouble Roams
Two Ghosts Haunt A Grove
Trick Or Treat Or Murder
Roses Are Red...He's Dead
Double, Double Nothing But Trouble

Mellow Summers moves to Vermont to attend college, accompanied by her friend Jackie. They soon find themselves running into ghosts and one mystery after another.

The Dystopia Trilogy

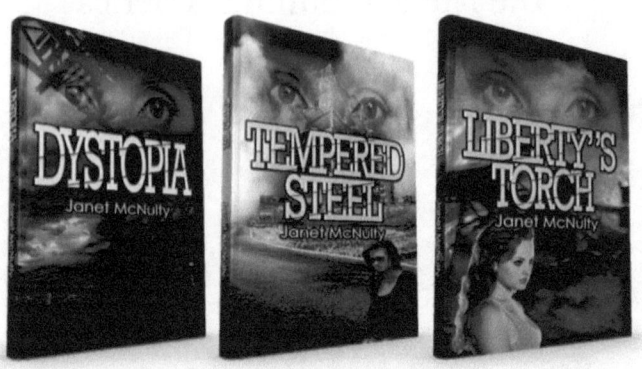

Dystopia (Book 1)
Tempered Steel (Book 2)
Liberty's Torch (Book 3)

**Imagine living in a world where
everything you do is controlled.**

Dana Ginary lives in a world where every aspect
of her life is controlled by the Dystopian Government.
Forced to work in Waste Management, her life becomes
a nightmare with hunger and survival is her only constant. Before she knows it, she is caught up in a resistance
movement and exiled from Dystopia, forced to find her
way in the barren wastelands. While there, she must learn
to live independently and discover how far she is willing
to go to live and achieve freedom.

The Solaris Saga

Solaris Seethes
Solaris Seeks
Solaris Strays
Solaris Soars

Every myth has a beginning

After escaping the destruction of her home planet, Lanyr, with the help of the mysterious Solaris, Rynah must put her faith in an ancient legend. Never one to believe in stories and legends, she is forced to follow the ancient tales of her people: tales that also seem to predict her current situation.

Forced to unite with four unlikely heroes from an unknown planet (the philosopher, the warrior, the lover, the inventor) in order to save the Lanyran people, Rynah and Solaris embark on an adventure that will shatter everything Rynah once believed.

The Legends Lost Series

Published under Nova Rose

Tesnayr
Amborese
Galdin

Enter the Lands of Tesnayr and join on an epic fantasy adventure that spans over 1,500 years.

Begin with Tesnayr, the first king of the five lands as he unites the against a savage foe bent on their destruction.

Next, Join Amborese as she fights reclaim the throne after her family was forced to flee from it.

Thinking peace has finally entered the land, follow Galdin as he returns to Tesnayr to find it greatly hanged. Barbarians, led by a mysterious sorcerer, burn and destroy as they go. And only Galdin can stop them if he chooses to accept his fate.

Visit www.legendslosttrilogy.com to learn more about the Legends Lost Trilogy.

Grandpa's Stories

My grandfather grew up in Arizona during the 1920s and 1930s. One week after the attack on Pearl Harbor he joined the Navy. During the summer of 2012, my mother visited him and recorded his stories about growing up, World War II, and his time as an employee at the Pacific Bell Telephone Company. This is the history of the 20th century as he lived it. These recordings make up this book. These are his words.